Ira Oberoi's Pursuit of Love

I0631623

Ira Oberoi's Pursuit of Love

NITI CHOPRA

Srishti
PUBLISHERS & DISTRIBUTORS

SRISHTI PUBLISHERS & DISTRIBUTORS
Registered Office: N-16, C.R. Park
New Delhi – 110 019
Corporate Office: 212A, Peacock Lane
Shahpur Jat, New Delhi – 110 049
editorial@srishtipublishers.com

First published by
Srishti Publishers & Distributors in 2018

*True love is hard to find, but once found
it changes your life forever.*

*This book is just a simple celebration
of one such crazy love.*

I was four years old when I heard my first love story ever.

'Jack and Jill went up the hill
To fetch a pail of water
Jack fell down and broke his crown
And Jill came tumbling after.'

It was short, sweet and simple. To me, it was perfect.

Jack and Jill became and remained my favourite love story.

Until, I came across ours.

Thanks, Hugs & Kisses

RR; for crafting a story as beautiful as ours.

Mom; for loving us unconditionally, just like we love you back.

Dad; for being the coolest, superbly unconventional dad ever.

Saarthoo; for being my all time partner-in-crime.

Vi; for being my twin-soul on earth.

Students from BRAC; for urging me to begin writing.

Friends from KDC and DIAS; for no reason, because being good friends is reason enough.

The team at Srishti; for all the patience and guidance.

And of course
Jai – Your green eyes are the only jewels that make this woman happy – I love you.

Prologue

Raindrops were falling.

The song that I had been listening had just ended, as had the day. Night was settling in and I felt too tired to pull out my phone for another song.

The bus was silent now. Mostly everyone had fallen asleep.

I sat leaning against the window pane, as tiny droplets hit the glass. One droplet merging into another and then another, till they all became a long streak, being stretched by the wind gushing across.

That's how everything felt in life.

One action leading to the next, to the next and so on. Circumstances pushing and pulling you, till the point you don't even realize where you are going.

Where was I going?

It was pouring in heavily now and I could barely see the road ahead.

Why was I here on this bus?

Did I really know what I wanted?

Was this even right?

Bright lights reflected sharply from the traffic coming towards us, forcing me to close my eyes. As I shut them, dreaded scenes from the past flashed randomly.

Mom was pacing up and down the living room, mumbling incoherently or maybe I was just too numb to understand what she was saying. I tried to blink away my tears, and as I wringed my hands I was shocked by her sudden outburst.

"I knew I'd have a heart attack in my life!" She was exasperated!

"Mumma, please relax!" I tried keeping my voice calm.

On the inside I was breaking apart but outside I couldn't let her see it.

I opened my eyes, fighting not to remember the scene.

I turned my head back to the window pane. The droplets were frenzied now, as they ran across the glass in full torrent.

They seemed to be angry, just like she was that night.

"What shame!

What had I expected from my daughter and this is what I have today! We spent lakhs in trying to make you a doctor... A respectable person... And this is what you do in college?! How could you?! I tried to make you a strong girl and you let yourself be used by a boy?!

You have failed me as a daughter! I feel sick when I am reminded of the things that you have done! Horrible!

Oh, I knew my health wasn't going to keep up... It was written since long in my destiny. But how was I to know my very own daughter was going to be the reason behind it!

What a shame! I cannot even imagine doing these things with a stranger. And you have gone ahead and... God damn it! How could you?!"

Tears were flowing freely now, onto my cheeks and into my hands.

A gush of wind slapped across my face forcing my eyes open.

Someone up front had opened a window. The fresh smell of rain mixed with wet mud twirled up my nostrils and I inhaled deeply the therapeutic concoction.

The person sitting right in front of me didn't seem to appreciate it and shouted out, insisting that the window be closed. Half a minute later, the world outside of the bus was shut out again and the creepy silence returned.

The same kind that had prevailed at home that fateful night. The silence before the storm.

"I can't take this anymore! This is just too much!"

I looked up and saw her swaying a little. I rushed to her side and caught hold of her just in time.

"I fear if Papa gets to know all this! He will surely kill you! Oh, God!"

"Mumma, please relax. It's all over now. Please," I pleaded meekly, speaking up for the first time since she had come.

But she wasn't listening to me.

"I did everything that I could for you and this is how you reward me! By failing me! By killing me!"

She took a deep breath and tightly grasped her chest, right over her heart. Her eyes wincing in pain she fell back onto the couch.

"Mumma! Mumma! Mumma!"

HONK! HONK!

I jumped out of my skin as a truck passed by, honking as if it was about to burst.

I had to stop thinking about that night. This was too much to handle on a trip like this. I had done what I had done.

I shook my head, wondering as to why in the first place had I decided to be a part of this show. With all the images of that dreaded day coming back, I felt I had made another mistake.

I took a few deep breaths trying to relax. Straightening up I pulled back my hair, trying to tie it into a ponytail. With one hand holding my hair, I bent over to pick up my bag, in need of a band.

For the last few days, I just couldn't seem to find anything. I was perpetually lost and confused. I wondered how I had even managed to appear for the end terms.

The bus trudged over a big speed breaker, without breaking its speed obviously, and my bag fell to the ground.

Shit!

I scrambled to pick up the loitered stuff.

Thank God everyone was sleeping!

I quickly picked up everything and settled back into my seat.

Nothing was happening right. And it was getting on my nerves. I placed back all the stuff into my bag, suddenly remembering the band was in a side pocket. Opening the pocket, I sighed as I saw the band but froze as I saw something else.

Slowly, almost reluctantly, I pulled out the little white box. Of all days, today it had to come up before me?

I sat there staring at the closed box as a new set of images flashed before my open eyes.

A couple – laughing, swinging on a see-saw, just returned from college.

An empty plate from the Chinese Van tossed near-by with a bottle of Coke.

So happy! Joking and laughing as the merry-go-round turned slowly.

Silently strolling across the park, hand in hand, as the winds whispered secrets of its own.

Playing with puppies, they had sheltered away from the unexpected rain.

The girl sitting on the bench, while the guy resting his head in her lap, gazing up into her face.

He pulled in and they kissed in the rain.

I blinked as tears filled my eyes, bringing me back to the bus.

The rain drops were dancing softly on the window.

Brushing away my tears with the back of my hand, I gently opened the box.

Inside lay a pair of lenses – green lenses.

I smiled, letting my tears flow freely now.

As an image of a face crossed my mind, I felt warm inside. With every drop that fell onto my lap, I could feel the agony being squeezed out of my heart.

It felt so good. It made me feel so much better.

The eyes were looking at me – emerald green eyes, sparkling with love.

Resting my head back against the seat, I let myself free – free to go back to where it had all started.

Free to revisit the beginning of the journey I was on.

Free to go back to the charm that had put me where I was today.

Free to go back to him.

Free to go back to his green eyes.

Roughly an year ago

The wind gushed across my face and it had started to lose sensation as I could barely feel the drop of tear that trickled down my cheek.

We zoomed along the almost empty lanes on some highway towards the place that would in much probability be called college.

My hair, that I had deliberately left open for no obvious reason except to rebel my own disciplinary super ego state, twirled about as if in a hyper magnetic trance.

It was a fine morning the month of September.

The sun was just the perfect yellow with the skies painted the loveliest of blues. Speckled across were tufts of clouds that looked like fresh whipped cream.

I gazed up and started imagining mythological characters from books that might one day be written – the giant with an elephant's tail, the ship with a hundred giraffes, the big eyed laughing clown, the mountain with a belly and arms – and it felt as if they were laughing, staring down at some loser on earth.

That loser being me!

Yes, the biggest loser on the planet. That is simply how I felt.

Born and brought up as the prodigy child – best at everything, more than perfect; an achiever par excellence. Bedazzled with the dreams of becoming a doctor right from a very early age, I aced academics all through schooling years and was ensured rigorous coaching to clear the medical exams.

Nothing worked though.

I did not even crack a single entrance out of more than a dozen that I had religiously appeared for. To top it all, pining complete hope and confidence on Medicine, I had not even planned a backup. That left me with no option for graduation.

I was doomed.

I dipped down deep into the passenger seat of the car, sneakily trying to wipe the trail that the rolling tear had left behind.

Out of the corner of one eye I could see Dad driving steadily at the maintained speed – his face expressionless as always, incomprehensible. There was no hint revealing the tornado of emotions that might be swirling inside his hard exterior. An epitome of wisdom and an aura that transcended peaceful vibes, Dad had been my hero since the day I could remember.

The road seemed to be endless – one straight stretch toward the place that I might be trudging towards half-heartedly for a good couple of years to follow.

What was it again?

Jagmohan College of Dental Sciences – JCDS.

Gosh!

I wish I was dead.

To think of it, had I even for a single moment in my life given a thought towards this decision of wanting to become a doctor?

Or was it just the usual parent induced aspiration that I wanted to make come true.

If hidden desires were to be explored, I had secretly wanted to become a florist, the pretty young lady at the counter full of fresh flowers – lilies and tulips and begonias and orchids and the all time favourite roses. A blooming, sweet smelling, completely oozing with honey flower shop that they showed in romantic Hollywood movies, that's where I wanted to be.

Yes, that bunch of clouds over the horizon also looked like white carnations with the daffodil sun mellowing behind them.

A sharp turn to the left and the entire scenery was robbed of me, as the car came to a halt.

A dull building with an even duller ambience stood in front of me – the loneliest place that could ever be.

This was going to be college.

My disappointment might well have been very obvious on my face as Dad gently placed one hand on mine and smiled.

"Let's go?"

I faked meek excitement and tiptoed out of the car.

It felt as if I was all of three years again, going to school for the first time in life when all I wished to do was just snuggle back into the warmth of my comforter and fly away to the land of chocolate clouds and milky rainbows.

I looked up.

The building was not huge. In fact I would rather say it was small for a college.

I shuffled along while Dad took his trademark long steps, brisk as always, and we headed towards the reception.

It was reasonably well maintained, though I could have never believed it to be a dental college entrance had I known otherwise. I could see an office on my left, a little door behind the lady sitting at the desk and a gallery that extending into mystery land on the right. A fleet of stairs twirled over the extreme left corner of the room and curved over onto what seemed to be the first floor.

Dad asked for someone in particular and we found that we needed to meet him in the adjacent building. Half an hour later, having finalized all the financials, we were given the honour of touring my soon to be college.

I strolled through the departments and the lecture theatres in a daze that seemed more like a nightmare of some kind, and finally, after what seemed like an eternity, we were back to the car.

Dad politely shook hands with the little person who was supposed to be the mediator for my admission and we drove off, back onto the road that was to take us home.

After a long silence that stretched for miles finally came Dad's question.

"So, are you sure?"

My mind reeled back to the solitary tree that I had noticed in the park just outside the reception at the college.

A single lonely tree that did not belong there at all, yet its destiny had somehow landed it in the midst of an environment so different.

I was the same tree. And destiny had planned the same for me.

I took a deep breath and smiled trying to assure him once again that I was not feeling like a loser – maybe I was just trying to reassure myself. Everything would be fine I hoped and with as much zeal that I could muster I finally said it out.

"Yes. I'm sure."

Dad smiled back and went back into his driving trance.

My fate was sealed.

A dentist was what I was fated to be.

Almost a month had passed and as I sat on the finely arranged seats in my daily anatomy lecture I felt a strange sense of rebellion seeping in. I had all of my life been the disciplined, always perfect, ever so correct and decent, all time sincere girl. And sitting on the desk of this privately owned dental college I could feel myself becoming like a completely nerdy dentist.

The thought completely freaked me out!

No! I wasn't going to allow it to happen and in a moment of self-realization I resolved to live up my college years to the hilt. I made a mental list of my resolutions:

First and foremost, I will not volunteer for any committee. Bearing the responsibilities of head girl in school had been enough.

I will be carefree and outgoing for once, forgetting about the perfect girl that my parents had reared me into.

I will....

What else? I wondered.

The professor was supposed to be teaching us about the number of bones and muscles in our body. She began enumerating the bones in our arms and I temporarily put my thoughts on hold.

She was one of the sweetest teachers I had ever met – at an age of fifty or more she was brimming with super energy. She was beautiful; red rosy cheeks, full of health and the warmest smile I had ever seen on any face. Her eyes glittered with such inflictive enthusiasm while she taught that you *wanted* to learn and her confidence was so contagious that she made sure every student in the class grasped anatomy to the bone.

Literally!

As she moved on to the bones of the hand, she asked us all to put up one palm outwards so that we could practically touch and feel the bones for better remembrance.

Ma'am went on and started marking the bones on the chart as we followed suit, by holding them on our outstretched palms – carpals, metacarpals, phalanges. I turned my hand, trying to feel the bones better, when I noticed the door open between my ring finger and pinkie.

One blink and my whole world came to a screeching halt.

My eyes remained fixed upon the door, magnetized with what had just caught my attention.

A slim face with the sexiest cuts, radiating a strangely peaceful glow, silky hair falling across the forehead and deep set eyes that seemed to pierce across the room right through my hand – a pair of bright green eyes.

I was completely dazed.

Was this happening for real? Or was I just hallucinating under the effect of the 'flexa flexa' spell that I had just run on me a couple of minutes ago?!

He spoke something of which I could not comprehend a word and the professor gestured him inside.

Oh my! I thought I would faint. This angelic figure of amazing sexiness would murder me to death just by the moves in his walk. Definitely taller than six feet, super finely cut in body he walked in with a sway that took my breath away.

What was happening to me?

I was this respectable girl from a very decent family who had never eyed guys – least to say in the ravishing manner that I was tempted to feast upon this particular one.

And almost as if my thoughts had been too loud, my neighbour hushed into my ear "Don't even think about it. He's committed."

I was too hypnotized by the weirdly new sensation that I was experiencing and her words failed to register on my mind.

"Would you?"

Ah! The pleasure of hearing to the sweetest music on earth seemed bland before the baritone of this heavenly descendant who was now staring directly at me.

The class starting cheering in unison!

Had he asked me to marry him?!

Before I could make any sense, my feet started walking. I was spell bound under the gaze of the green eyes.

With every inch that I stepped closer, the intensity in his eyes seemed to pierce deeper into my heart.

My breath deepened and I could feel my legs shivering beneath me. But I could not stop myself. My legs took me straight up to him and barely inches away from where the God of Cupid stood, I stopped.

His eyes hadn't left mine even for a second and now that I stood so close, I could see that they were a perfect shade of emerald, hidden with secrets I was already dying to know.

He threw a smile at me – the sexiest of sexy smiles that my heart caught like the trophy of a lifetime.

"Who else?"

He asked to the class, looking at no one in particular.

What?! Was this a group marriage?!

Now that I stood facing a class full of a hundred students, I came back to my senses with a jolt, the realization of reality around me seeping in slowly.

This was no marriage proposal!

"Anyone else who wants to volunteer for the college committee?" blared out a plump girl from the team standing around me.

And how did I end up volunteering for the post?!

Oh, it must have been my frozen hand that had refused to go down under the hypnosis of the flexa flexa and Cupid combo of magic.

Well, I might as well take advantage of the situation, I ventured daringly.

I inched a step closer judging how much taller he was than I was. I would have to look up to his angel face with my head tilted backward while he leaned in to kiss me.

Perfect!

As I stood beside him, the scent of his cologne reached me teasingly, intoxicating me into ecstasy.

Gosh! Here I was standing before an audience of a hundred would be doctors, unconsciously having volunteered myself for the post of executive in the college committee under this guy's spell and not even knowing his name, I had already started fantasizing about him.

What had happened to me?!

Amidst the cheering of my newly found batch-mates, standing in the aura of this love tower beside me, I felt I had completely disintegrated from the very depth of my reasoning.

The class cheered louder!

I had won in the show of hands – chosen for the post of executive.

I felt elated and smiling like a crazy child I looked up into the green eyes of hidden wonders and once again the world around me became hazy.

He leaned in slightly towards me, flashing an amazingly sexy smile that I would probably never have enough of.

"Congratulations."

I could almost feel his breath under my ear and a thrill went down my spine.

I was completely and disastrously smitten.

The trees passed by like a blur of paint as our van zoomed past the very straight road that connected my college and home.

But today felt so much more beautiful.

The clouds looked softer, the sun felt warmer, the flowers on the road seemed to be happier and every gush of wind bought along a new fragrance that was filling my heart in abundance – the fragrance of love.

And to think of it, I had been smitten at first sight!

My heart pounded as I remembered the events of the previous day.

I could just close my eyes and it seemed not a second had passed since I had met the Greek God of Love. Gosh! I could feel myself getting dizzy again with the strange kind of feeling that had baffled me yesterday in the lecture theatre too.

Was this really love? Is this how it was supposed to feel?

Or was I actually just catching the flu?!

"Are you all right?"

My friend, Kriti put her hand over my shoulder and as I turned to face her I caught myself smiling like an idiot in the rear view mirror. So, that is why she must have asked!

"Yeah, I'm fine! Just kind of was reminded about a funny incident."

Look at me! I just couldn't stop grinning!

For what?! Why was I so happy?!

For God's sake, I didn't even know his name yet!

And just as I thought of how crazy I was going, the van turned into the gates of college which had suddenly become the loveliest place on the planet.

The excitement to come to college and meet Him again had almost killed me!

The van screeched to a halt and I rushed towards the reception, without waiting for Kriti and the others, my eyes in search of the face that had taken my breath away.

I slowly scanned the entire hall way down till the ends, a wee bit sad at not finding him.

As if I had been expecting him to be waiting for me!

Slowly I trudged towards my class in the basement.

"Hey! Really excited about today's lecture?"

Kriti had just caught up and as she saw me she came to a standstill.

"What? Is everything okay? You look a little lost."

Me and my face! Why did it have to be so overtly expressive?!

"Ya! Ya! I'm absolutely fine!"

I must have been subconsciously still searching for Angel face because my friend burst out laughing. She started to drag me towards the other side of the basement hallway. The lights there were still not on, and I could barely see where I was going!

"Hey! But our class is that side, not here!" I exclaimed, not the least worried about the lecture as I had better, much lovelier things on my mind!

Wide eyed, and sincere to the end, she locked her eyes into mine.

"I know you're searching for *Him*! The two of you would look so lovely, so absolutely perfect together! You're made for each other. The moment I saw you on stage with Him yesterday, I knew it! It is so obvious in your eyes, babe! You're in love!"

I was dazed! I could feel the warmth of my blush all over my face as I realized I was smiling at her.

She took my hands and lead to the turn at the hallway.

Just across was a door.

"He's in there" She tilted her head towards Lecture Theatre 3 and my light bulb struck aglow.

Of course!

He was my senior, so he had to be in this lecture hall. Seniors started their classes an hour earlier than us.

The hallway and the theatre, everything was dark, except for the light coming from the over head projector inside the class. It was too dim for me to be able to see anything and had I taken a step forward it would surely make me visible to the ones sitting inside.

I decided against it.

Turning back to face Kriti, I beamed gleefully. She was so happy for me! And me, I was ecstatic.

I caught Kriti's hand and we ran back towards our own class, hoping to reach before the scheduled lecture's professor reached. We zoomed past the staircase, the feared lecturer's shadow in the periphery of our vision, skidding through the doorway, right across the steps straight up to the last row. Panting hard we quickly turned into our seats as the class rose in unison, to wish the lecturer who had just entered the room.

"Good morning, class! Take your seats!" she called out loudly.

Phew! Saved by a whisker!

Or so I thought, a second too soon.

"And the girls, who came running into the room before me, please keep standing."

Damn!

The entire class turned towards us, at the last seat of the class and we paused in mid air, deciding whether to accept or not. I stood up straight and pulled up Kriti too.

We had just been running in the corridor, so what was there to be afraid of? We definitely were not in kindergarten to be restricted from loitering around in the hallway.

"Were you the ones who came running past me in the corridor?" The lecturer asked in a stern voice.

"Yes ma'am, it was us." I admitted, rather over confidently!

That is how I had always been. No matter what, I was confident in the right as well as the little itsy-bitsy wrong that I had ever done.

"Well, you had better start to behave like a doctor!"

Short, crisp and icy the words rang across the room and reached us like a cane. As she started to teach, we both slunk down deep into our chairs. Slowly but surely, some wicked charm of the evil forces, came over us. I was going mad trying to control my laughter while Kriti had literally turned red trying to control hers!

Behave like a doctor?!

Seriously, this had to be the most amusing thing I had ever heard in the last two months of college. With all the adrenaline rush and excitement that was bursting inside of me, the taunt seemed to be the funniest joke ever! With immense struggle we tried to calm ourselves down, not wanting to get ourselves into any further trouble. God only knows how we passed that lecture without bursting into splits.

That happened as soon as the lecturer left our room.

When finally we came back to reasonably sound senses, I looked at Kriti and even before I could ask, she smiled.

"He *is* the one for you" she blurted out, thrilled with delight.

Kriti started laughing again and hugged me tight.

"Let's check out their class again," I suggested.

We once again ran across the corridors, not once behaving like doctors that we had been so seriously warned about and reached Lecture Theatre 3. My anticipation was touching the roof as we turned around the corner.

But alas! The room was empty! Nevertheless, the newly found hope was much to look forward to.

College was no longer the boring old building that I had barely explored in the past few days. It was no longer a substitute for what I had not been able to get.

It was no longer a compromise. It was destiny.

This was *the* place – the place where I had to meet Him.

My angel with green eyes.

For the next few days, the entire anatomy of mine kept searching my Greek God – my eyes kept wandering through the lecture halls across the basement, my feet kept me running through the corridors at all odd hours, my hands kept me busy writing some dreamy poetry that I wished my heart would understand.

I was crazier, naughtier and so much happier than I had ever been before! I kept smiling all through the day and the nights had never felt so longer – I was surely becoming a lunatic.

Such is love's sweet poison.

Just one dose is enough to turn a perfectly normal human being into a crazy lunatic craving for more and more.

I was love's latest victim.

After a long wait of nineteen days, my chance of seeing him again was revived. Our first official meeting for the College Committee was to take place.

The plump Deepa Ma'am, turned out she was the Secretary of the Committee, came in to announce that all members had to stay back. A meeting had been scheduled at the end of the day in Lecture Theatre 3.

I let out a long deep sigh to calm down my pounding heart.

Every passing hour seemed like a milestone achieved. My heart had been pining to get even a glimpse since that fortunate day, so the announcement of the meeting was like a saviour for me – a drop of nectar for my thirsty soul.

I was so excited to see Him, I could barely sit down for a minute!

Finally, the drone like voice of the professor came to a halt and as names were called out for attendance, the class started coming out of its deep slumber.

We had classes post lunch in a super cooled lecture theatre with all lights dimmed completely – apparently to aid the OHP displaying the professor's presentation – but in reality aiding us all get to sleep. The monotonous humdrum of the professor additionally acted as a background lullaby.

But today, instead of the usual slumber, I was in dream land imagining what my angel was going to look like.

As the clock struck four, I was the most alert of all in the class, desperate for the lecture to end! Finally, after like what seemed an eternity, the professor managed to get together all her files and documents and what not, leaving the room after reminding us for the umpteenth time about the assignments that we had to submit next week.

For God's sake, lady! Chillax!

You'll get your assignments, all right on time! Now leave!

As I stood up my eyes followed her to the gate. And then it happened. My heart skipped a beat, or maybe stopped beating completely as I forgot to breathe at all.

Ma'am walked out. Angel walked in.

It had only been a few days since I had last seen him, but a mere glimpse of his face amongst the crowd of students leaving the room was enough to turn my world out of balance! My eyes refused to blink, my knees started to sway, my stomach was suddenly the stage of dancing butterflies and my heart decided to pump all my body's blood into my face.

Somehow, I pulled myself out of the pleasurable trance and started walking. As I was starting to regain my senses, I noticed the other students who had walked in with Him – I presumed them all to be committee members as well.

Ms. Plump was there too – talking loudly to anyone and everyone who was there around her.

My angel was just like I remembered him – quite, calm and poised. A very determined and serious look on his angelic face – oh, his face...

How I would have loved to stroke a finger over that jaw line and across the sharp chin bone... Brrrrrrrrr!

As I reached the front two rows, I realized that Ms. Plump was calling all the new members to the very front – that included me.

I took one deep breath and with usual confidence strode up and stood right in front of her, fully aware of the fact that his eyes were following me all along. I deliberately avoided looking towards him and smiled a little nod at Ms. Plump.

I knew his eyes were still on me as I could feel the energy radiating toward me, and as soon as Ms. Plump returned my nod, I didn't waste a millisecond to turn towards him. A pair of the most beautiful green eyes I had ever seen caught mine.

There was just a faintest of faint smile on his face, or maybe it was a big smile – I wouldn't have known, because my eyes were just too transfixed on the green gems that were holding my gaze with so much strength.

He nodded briefly, and then broke away his gaze, going on to greet my other batch-mates.

I smiled and lowered my head, as I could feel my cheeks glowing again.

Quietly I slipped into the first row and while all the introductions were being done, I reached the seat which I hoped would be the closest to the centre. Deep in my heart, I positively believed that the President would obviously address the committee from the centre.

I was right!

Completing the formal nods to all the newbies, he walked right towards the front of my seat and paused at just about arm's length from the row.

I was unconditionally owned.

"Hello, everyone"
His voice was crisp and firm.

"I'm Raaghav and I'm the committee President. I welcome all the new executive members from the first year into the college committee."

To me although, it sounded like music – I could listen to the sound of his voice all day!

He introduced Ms. Plump and a few other members, but my eyes were fixed on the only green eyes in the room.

Clear, filled with light and warm to the core, they sparkled like jewels.

As he went on to state the few basic functions of what the committee exactly does, my eyes could just not move anywhere except for his face and I sat in my chair numbed by this strange feeling that had gotten into me.

I could feel his energy around me and I wanted to know more about him. I wanted to hang out with him, talk to him, look into those green eyes and know him. I wanted to touch that face and feel the warmth beneath my hands.

I shuddered at the thought of being so close to him and goosebumps spread all over my arms. As I slid my arms beneath the table, my movement must have caught his eye. He looked directly at me and our eyes met.

He paused in his speech.

For a few seconds that seemed almost like an eternity, he simply continued to look at me – the moment of the day, one that I would replay over and over again.

I wished time to stop. But of course that was not to happen.

"Is it too cold for you in here?"

Pulling my arms beneath must have made him think so... Aw! How sweetly considerate!

My smile widened.

"I'm perfectly fine, thanks!" I replied politely.

And then came the smile that made my heart flip over twice and I realized the power that it held. In an instant, I knew it for sure, that I would do just about anything to see that smile again and again.

Who would believe, the girl who had been famous for making guys go head over heels and not giving a damn about it, was today hopelessly disarmed, by a mere smile.

The meeting did not last long and I didn't catch much except a few words about the competitions to be held in the following weeks.

For all of the twenty five minutes that it lasted, I was completely mesmerized by my Angel and not even for a second did I dare to take my eyes off Him.

And this surely must not have gone unnoticed.

⌘

Week 1

The contests for Week 1 and the hustle bustle in the college was not enough to distract me.

Every morning my day would begin searching for him in his lecture theatre – where I rarely found him! Occasionally, I would see him on rounds supervising the events – one sighting near the Rangoli Competition, another one near Face Painting.

But the mere glimpses that I could manage were far from satiable and I craved for more.

He was super duper busy! Running from one event to the other, handling the competitions, managing the judges, settling scores and what not!

We executives were new to the committee – our only duty was to observe and report anything important to our seniors, so I did not get too many chances to stay with the core team that surrounded Mr President.

On top of that, Kriti had given our names in the Salad Making competition which was to last for more than an hour – that meant lesser time for me to stalk my man!

Reluctantly, I dragged my feet inside the hall where our event was about to begin. Kriti had already set up the table and was arranging all the ingredients – jumping with excitement. Her enthusiasm was infectious and I chipped in, humming the romantic track that I had been listening to for the last two weeks on loop.

"He's not coming to this event," Kriti quipped, as I flipped over some radishes.

I raised my hands and shrugged my shoulders, pretending I was lost. My mind, on the other hand, was already working in full tempo – he visits every event when the judges are in the process of marking, so he would be coming to this one as well! That means I would be getting a chance to see him!

"You can't fool me dear. You know who I'm talking about," she gently cooed as she cleaned the bowls and placed them on side of the large table.

"Who's not coming?" I asked sheepishly, tugging my ear as I tried to hide my blushing face.

She put down her precious bowls and stood facing me, one hand on her waist and one on the table.

"You know who one of our judges is – The senior professor from Prostho. And everyone knows the equation between him and your dreamboat is far from amicable. So, quit dancing around in the hope of seeing him here and start focusing on this!"

She picked up a big water melon and propped it right into my hands. It did not feel as heavy as my heart had suddenly become.

Kriti shook her head and smiled.

"But you do know that the results are all collated by the committee president which means...."

"Which means we *have to* win this event!" I blurted out in a shout.

We both giggled like two little girls and with renewed enthusiasm I returned to arranging our weapons – fruit peeler, vegetable grater....

This was another chance to get my name in his eyes, literally. I wanted him to know my name and this seemed like a good way around it....

Lemon squeezer, mixer, pepper shaker....

We had to win this event, no matter what....

Salad fork, fruit fork, table spoons and toothpicks! There! All set to win the battle!

I clasped my hands together, and took a final glance at the cutlery admiring my own arrangement. Wait a minute!

I glanced again into the bag and checked the table once again, but I couldn't find it.

"Aaaaaaaa.... You did put in our main weapon, right?" I asked my friend as I started poking her arm incessantly.

"Main *weapon*?" she enquired apparently confused.

"How are we supposed to go to battle in a salad completion without it?"' I waived my hand showcasing the missing member from our cutlery.

She still did not get it, though! I threw up my hands in the air.

"The knife! We don't have a knife!"

The dramatist in me played on in full spirit.

"We're doomed! How can we possibly win a salad-making competition without a knife?"

I sank down into a chair.

"What are we going to do now, gal? We've lost the battle even before we could begin," I resisted the urge to laugh at myself.

Kriti calmly placing the bowls and trays, nudged me sharply and I squealed!

"Owww!"

"If your melodramatic act of resigning from the war is finished, would you now like to get up and get the knives from the canteen? I gave them to Bhaiya in the morning so that he could get them sharpened for us," she casually stated, absorbed in her polishing of glass.

I grinned, as I vaguely remembered her mentioning this in the morning.

I hugged her before running away to retrieve our precious knives from the canteen.

As I walked past the corridors, the hope of seeing him again rekindled – I was again in the realms of events.

I darted past the reception towards the lawns that separated the main building from the canteen. The volleyball event was going on in the lawn and as I recalled from memory the number of players on each side of the net, I stopped in mid track.

There on the volleyball court, playing centre forward was none other than the guy who had robbed me of my sensibility!

One look at him was enough to disrupt all thought processes in my mind – to pace my heart beats in multiples – to shallow my breathing – to warm me from the inside – to make me go *absolutely* crazy!

And as if by magnetic attraction, my feet started walking towards the game. Like a zombie, fixated to the playing figure of my angel, I sauntered across the road, into the lawns.

The stupid smile on my face had returned for good.

A player from the other side hit the ball attempting to slam into Angel's side but my hero – ah! The master player of his time – dived and raised the ball back into the opponent's court in a clean sweep that they had not anticipated.

Score point!

I clapped enthusiastically, my face beaming in glee.

My applause must have been quite loud as a few players on the court turned towards the audience, and so did he! As he high fived his buddy on the court, he glanced across right at me!

Our eyes met for just a second, as he passed a hand through his hair, settling them back momentarily, before he returned to his stance in the game.

He was smiling for sure – I could bet my life on it!

My heart warmed up. I sighed in deep contentment and mesmerized by his moves, watched the game intently – rather watched *him* closely.

He wasn't too muscular, rather skinny but he definitely had strong arms and shoulders. I could see a subtle bulge of bicep muscle under the sleeves of his t-shirt whenever he pulled himself up in the air for his shots. Agility and flexibility were apparent by the smooth game that he played. He surely was the tallest of the lot – more than six feet without a doubt!

The game went on and I was lost in indulgence.

Lost in my thoughts, ranging from mildly sweet to bluntly naughty, I was oblivious to the world around me, when suddenly I realized that my phone was ringing. Absent minded, I picked up the call not bothering to see the caller.

"Hello?" I sang softly into the phone. Only to be shocked by the shout that came from the other end!

"Where are you?! The knives! I need them – our event started twenty five minutes ago! I'm done with all the peeling and shredding! Are you manufacturing the knives? I just asked you to bring them?! And you vanish into thin air! Where are you?!"

I was already on my feet, rushing to the canteen. Our event had absolutely been erased from my mind – what event, everything had been erased from my mind!

"Reaching in a second," I whispered into the phone before disconnecting the call.

I barged into the canteen, shouting out for the knives to Bhaiya who already had them ready in one corner.

"Hello beta! They've been ready since morning as I thought you're event was supposed to start earlier," he quipped looking at his watch.

"Yes yes, bhaiya!" I blurted, hurriedly picking up the basket of knives from the counter. "There was some change in the plan of events," I added meekly.

"Thanks a lot!" I shouted out loud as I ran out of the door.

I couldn't help but resist – it might be the last look for the day – I justified to myself and caught him having water in a huddle near the nets.

He saw me too.

Taking another gulp from the sipper he continued to watch me and in all my heart's desire I wanted to keep contact – but the basket of weapons in my hands was too risky and I had to break contact with his gaze to watch where I was placing my feet. As I settled the basket a bit more comfortably into my arms, I looked up and my heart skipped a beat – he was still looking at me!

Hands crossed over one another, he was leaning against the pole with one leg bent at the knee and the foot resting backwards on the pool. The sun was shining graciously on this divine beauty of a person making his hair glow a brilliant brown.

It took all the strength that I had to quicken my pace and break the gaze that I was so gladly enjoying... I rushed across, my heart at dizzying height of happiness.

He was looking at me!

I broke into a little jig of joy!

Running into our event, I placed the basket right beside the big pile of nude veggies that she had prepared.

"I'm sorry!" I gave one of my sweetest smiles and added. "Come, let's win this event!"

She smiled, giving me a knowing look and I picked a big knife to place into her hands.

"C'mon, c'mon! Start chopping gal! You've already wasted a lot of time!" I said placing a denuded melon right before her.

"You!" She posed to stab me with the knife and the two of us burst out laughing.

"I am going to kill you after the competition but for now I need a clean knife," she blurted within bursts of laughter.

"Of course!" I replied, as I picked up another knife and started slicing a red pepper. "Kill me once I've got the medal from Mr President." I grinned at her.

She winked back at me before getting back to the melon.

I mustered all the focus that I could as I saw her determination. She ought to win this event and I had to give my best for her.

Full of purpose, I poured my heart into creating the finest salad on earth for my dear friend. Had it not been for her knives, I wouldn't have had the time of a lifetime.

I owed her one.

Two hours and lots of creative work later, we gratified ourselves in our masterpiece amidst immense appreciation from the participants around us. We had bagged the second prize and Kriti was delighted beyond reason. I was glad – definitely for my sweet gal who was basking in the glory of her culinary skills but more so because now my name was in one of the lists that *'he'* would be scrutinizing.

The thought of Raaghav knowing my name gave me a weird sense of pleasure. Smug with satisfaction and happy with my accomplishments of the day, I started packing to retire for home. It had been a really interesting day – the longest I had ever got to see him. And more importantly, for the first time today, I had caught him staring back at me.

The next week unfortunately, turned out to be a more challenging one. Every day I would loiter outside his lecture hall, spend hours at a stretch in the canteen and roam around uselessly in the corridors but to no avail.

Each evening I would return home a little more dejected than the previous and lock myself into my study pretending to be absorbed in thick books of Anatomy and Physiology. But in actuality, all I could manage to do was pour my heart out into prose and poetry. I opened my diary and scribbled the date in the corner. I wanted to write but I felt too lost for words. I was missing him damn too much! Just once if I could have had a glimpse of that face... Or hear that voice... Just once!

Taking a deep breath, I folded my arms on the table and buried my head into a little cave of recluse. Closing my eyes tightly, I replayed the volleyball scene for a millionth time in my mind. Relishing the effect it had on me, I contemplated on disconnecting the call that was buzzing on my phone. Just as I picked it up, my mind decided to change teams and reluctantly I pressed the green button.

"Hello" I answered quietly into my mobile.

"Hello! Am I talking to Ira?"

My heart stopped beating and the world around me came to a standstill. I could recognize this voice even amidst the hubbub of a concert – the smoothness, the sheer sexiness, the cool attitude, the hidden warmth. I thanked God I was not standing as my knees felt weak like butter. It was *Him*!

"Yes?" I answered as flatly as I could, my heart in my throat, ready to jump out!

"Hi, Ira! I'm Raaghav, President of the college committee."

"Oh... Hi!" I faked a surprised reaction

"I hope you remember me?"

Awww, that was sweet! You pull the purpose of my existence around yourself and ask me whether I remember you?! Cool move, man! I decided to be cooler – let's flirt!

"Remember?! I haven't forgotten you since the day I saw you!" I cooed without restraint.

"Hmm-hmm...? I hope I'm not disturbing you."

"No! No! Not at all..."

"Well, I actually needed some help for the upcoming events this week."

"Sure! What can I do for *you*?" I asked, playfully stressing the word 'you'.

"Ummm... Let's see. I need twenty pairs of socks for the One-Minute event this Saturday. Would you be able to arrange that?"

"Of course!" I replied without even giving it a thought.

Socks... Shoes... Slippers... You name it baby! I'll arrange whatever you want!

"Are you sure? *Twenty pairs* – you'll be able to arrange them?"

"Ah, I don't need to *arrange* them... They're *already* arranged!" I sprinted across the room to my big bag of little garments – all my socks had to be in here.

"Okay, good. That's it. Bring them tomorrow so that things are set up for Saturday."

"Sure!"

"Thanks!"

"The pleasure is aaaaaallll mine," I sang into the phone, my flirtation apparent beyond doubt. There was a small pause and I don't know what made me believe he was smiling on the other side of the phone.

"Bye, Ira."

"Byeee..." I stretched it as beautifully as I could and the line went dead.

Our first conversation!

I couldn't believe it. I pinched myself twice. He had my number – that means he must have searched for it. *And* he knew my name! I fell back on the bed, holding my phone tightly to my chest. He could have called anyone for the socks, but he had decided on me.

My spirits had risen beyond the zenith and there was no calling them back. I quickly opened the phone log to save his number. The phone was asking me to enter the caller's name. I surely couldn't call him 'sir' as was tradition in dental colleges. I hadn't used Sir in our little talk right now as well. I smiled, recollecting that he hadn't seemed to mind it. I stared back into my phone. Simply typing in his name seemed too blunt.

Ah! I knew it, the perfect name – Dr Green Eyes.

After all, they were the culprit - the culprit behind the chaos in my heart.

A sudden urge to write overtook me. Words started flooding my thoughts and I grabbed my diary from the table, quickly scribbling on the open page.

Long nights seem to pass away in a blink and days become shorter than the breaths taken...

The soul finds peace, the heart is deemed restless as the serenity of the mind is utterly forsaken...

The yearning grows, faith in miracle strong and hope's desire blooms unshaken...

Outside the window, the skies had turned a rich golden in shade – the sun was setting. I could hear some birds chirping and as I watched, the clouds changed colour from light blue to bright orange and then to a soft golden yellow.

Dusk had fallen. I sighed. I loved dusk.

As the clouds settled into the shadows of the falling night, I could see a few stars twinkling above the horizon. Stars had the power to grant wishes. Though, I had read that in so many stories as a child, I had long outgrown the concept thanks to a veracious account of the solar system in the General Studies class.

But today, love-struck and wounded by cupid I stared at the brightest star that I could see from the window in my room and wondered, what if....

What if those stories actually had some magical truth in them? What if stars actually had the power to grant wishes?

I smiled at the star. It looked like a tiny diamond in the sky, just the way the kindergarten poem used to describe it.

And with a silent wish to the heavenly star I finished the last lines of my poetry...

And as dreams come to life with belief and patience; in the gift of true love do souls awaken... In the gift of true love do souls awaken

Bra. Hanky. Hanky. Panties. Panties. Bra. Bra. Slit. Hanky. Sock!

I quickly placed it one side of the bag separate from all the other stuff that I was retrieving.

Bra. Hanky. Bra. Bra. Sports Bra. Slit. Panties.

Sock! Sock!

That makes it one and a half pair. I continued searching.

Seriously!? Till today I had never realized how rich I was in terms of under garments but socks?! *One-and-a half pairs?!* This was ridiculous! And how confidently I had told him I'd get twenty pairs. Tomorrow!

Well done, gal! I smirked at myself. I glanced at my watch. It was 7:30 p.m. The market would still be open. In a jiffy, I grabbed my shrug and handbag and ran out of the room.

"I need to go to the market to buy some important stuff for tomorrow's lecture," I announced rushing across the living room to whosoever was cared to know.

I quickly hunted through the shoe rack outside the main door for all the possible socks that my other family members might have. I managed to find five and a half pairs – mostly Dad's. What was it with the socks in our house? I wondered as I skipped down the stairs. Incomplete pairs! So now I had 5.5 plus 1.5... seven pairs at home.

Twenty pairs of socks I had to get as my task – the first ever entrusted upon me. I wasn't going to miss this chance for a million dollars!

Determined, I set out to buy the remaining thirteen pairs of socks.

⌘

Week 2

It was starting to get cold in the basement and as I stood waiting outside his lecture hall I could feel the goose bumps on my arms. The stir inside caught my attention and I knew the lecture was over. I waited patiently for the professor to leave and just before I could make up my mind whether to enter the hall or wait for him to come outside, I was greeted by Deepa Ma'am aka Plumpy.

"Hey!"

"Hi! Umm... I had to give these socks...."

"Oh great!" she interrupted even before I could finish my sentence and almost snatched the bag of socks from my hand.

"Thanks sweetheart!" she added with a smile too sweet for my liking.

I contemplated whether I should be asking for Raaghav but Plumpy had just not gained my admiration yet. There was something about her that just didn't make me feel too comfortable.

I voted against it.

"My pleasure." I nodded curtly, my eyes on all the people leaving the hall behind her.

"Is the committee president around? I thought I'd just confirm whether the socks are fine or not. I was calling him last night, but I guess he must have been busy." I played around with the right words.

I had called him only twice but that was all my conscience had allowed me to. No answer and no revert till morning had challenged me to talk to him face-to-face and here I was.

"He's not here, dear... He is very busy. And if I were you, I'd stop wasting my time," she said all knowingly.

I maintained a blank face.

"He called you because he needed the work done. That's it. It's not like he's going to call you daily and chit chat for hours! What are you thinking?!" She sounded disgusted.

To hell with you Plumpy! I wanted to punch her in the face, "Yeah, well. Thanks... I have a class!"

I tried to retort back, unsuccessfully. Pocketing my jeans, I slowly walked away to my hall. I had been hit hard. I had no clue why Plumpy's words mattered so much but she had successfully forced my brain and heart into battle.

Brain (Logically) – Why did he do it, there must be a good reason?

Heart (Crying like a baby) – He doesn't want to talk to me!

Brain – Why did he call me and then not pick up my calls – must have gotten busy.

Heart – He is ignoring me!

Brain – He needed help and he thought I was reliable.

Heart (Ripping apart itself) – I am being used!

Aaarrrrgghhh! I was going crazy!

I had to shut this out and the only way was to clarify it. Get it cleared up from source – that's what I had always done.

I would have to wait though. Of all days in the world, today was when I had to forget my mobile at home. I wondered how the day would pass. But as the clock struck four, I felt kind of proud.

You don't want to talk to me? Fine! I don't care!

Triumphantly, I headed back home, without once searching for him in the corridor or the canteen.

As the cab zoomed by on the straight road home, I could hold my façade no more. I curled up my legs and buried my face into them. I felt like crying. This was ridiculous.

He had just called me up to get some socks. It was a professional call to get the committee work done. Where had he once said that he had called me up so that we could be friends? Why was I assuming? Why was I feeling hurt if he had not received my call? Why was I acting like such a big idiot?

I didn't even know what he thought about me. It was me who had been going all gaga over him.

My heart crushed under the gravity of its own ignorance, I entered my house and dragged my feet straight to my room – bolting it from the inside.

Throwing my stuff on the couch, I fell on my bed and closed my eyes shut – all I could see was Him.

His face... His smile... His green eyes.

Him standing in the canteen...

Walking across my lecture theatre...

Entering our class for the very first time...

Congratulations! He had said, giving me the enchanting smile that had robbed me of my peace.

And then he leaned in to kiss me! His lips on mine, soft as rose petals, sweet as honey, wet as morning dew – slowly he pulled me in as I lost myself in his arms.

⌘

Present day

Whoa!

My eyes sprang open as the bus came to a shrieking halt. My breathing was shallow and I took a long deep breath to calm myself. Imagining him... Imagining *us*... Still had the same effect on me...

I had never understood it then. And in many ways it was still mysterious to me.

I looked down at the box of lenses which was still in my hand. I had worn them only once. He hadn't liked them and so I had just let them be. Closing the box, as if it contained some precious jewels, I carefully stuffed it back in my bag.

It had stopped raining, but there was a major jam that we were caught in. I peered through the glass, as the traffic around us inched slowly. As the bus crawled a little further, a big hoarding caught my eye.

IF YOU NEED TO JUSTIFY, IT'S NEVER GOING TO WORK.

Of all the things in the world, this is what had to be written here?! Another sign or just coincidence?

The bus moved across it before I could make out what the advert was all about. Anyways, my mind was wheeling back to where I had just been snapped out from a few minutes ago.

'If you need to justify yourself to someone, it's never going to work'

Raaghav's voice, warm and soft, rang clearly in my ears as I closed my eyes again going back to my room.

Back to the day of our first special moment.

Back to Ira's room

I opened my eyes. I had to call him up. I needed to clear things out – if not for him, then definitely so for myself. In one quick move I jumped across the room, grabbing my phone and falling back on the bed. Only to rise again with surprise!

Four missed calls.

Despite my state of gloom, my heart was pinning to see just one name when I clicked it open.

And there it was! *Dr Green Eyes.*

For a minute I thought I was hallucinating. Was this really happening? I checked the call log. One missed call in the morning at 10, followed by another one at 10:02. A third one at 12:30 and a fourth one at 4:00 in the evening.

All the timings had been matched to when I might be expected to be free – that couldn't be co-incidence?! But what was he calling me for? Rather, why was he calling me in the first place?

Surely, for some official work right?!

Resolved to clear it up, I hit dial on the number and firmly put the phone to my ear. It didn't take too long for him to answer.

"Hey!" His calm voice filled in from the other end. It was easy to make out he was relieved. The unexpected concern made my heart flutter.

No, Ira! I cautioned myself. Don't get soft. He didn't call you back last night. He's not going to use you. Be firm.

"Hi."I kept it as blank as I could.

"Just returned from college?" he asked softly.

I decided to monkey around.

"Na! Had a conference to attend in Australia last night, just made it back to India," I quipped.

There was a soft laugh at his end. Had it been another day, I would have dropped all guard to listen to that voice again.

But today was not going to be so.

"I couldn't pick up your calls, last night. I'm sorry."

Oh, he sounded so sweet! So genuinely sweet and honest. I knew he had been calling me since morning to apologize. I knew it even before he said it.

"I was calling you since morning, but I guess you were busy," he added.

"I forgot my phone at home today," I quietly muttered.

"Oh!" He sounded amused. "Well, I'm really sorry for last night..."

"It's okay," I cut him off. "No problem."

Suddenly I was feeling so small. I had been imagining all sorts of things since morning and here he was – trying to reach me all day, just to apologize for not being able to take my calls.

There was silence. He didn't hang up.

"So, how was your day in college today? You sound tired."

What? I had just spent a good deal of my energy pestering myself over the thought that he wouldn't want to talk to me and here we were – trying to do small talk and mood analysis!

My day in college?! It went quite pathetic, thanks to you not being there! I was reminded of how Plumpy had ruined my morning. And something so strong came over me that I didn't even get a second to stop myself.

"I was told you wouldn't call me back and that you have no interest in talking to me," I blurted out.

"Hmmm...." He mused. "So that's why you sound so different than yesterday."

One talk with me was enough for him to know how I sounded when I was normal and what abnormal might constitute of? That was pretty nice. But I was not going to let my heart win over at the moment. I waited for him to say something in his favour – to answer – to justify – to agree, to disagree... Anything! But the silence continued.

"What?!" I cried into the speaker. "You've got nothing to say to that?"

"To what?" he asked, mildly confused.

"To what I was told by Deepa Ma'am, today!"

"Well, *I* didn't say that to you so who am I to comment on it." He hadn't been perturbed one bit – same calm voice.

"Ya, all right! But are you not going to justify yourself?!" I argued.

The same soft laugh.

"No, I don't need to justify myself. If you need to justify yourself to someone, it's never going to work," he said softly, as if trying to explain a very crucial mechanism of Physiology.

"And *this*...." He paused. "This I *want* to work."

My heart literally stopped beating.

The ray of hope that I had caught in his 'This I want to work' phrase was like an entire sun shining upon me.

He wanted this to work!

Of course, my well calibrated brain had been in continuous analysis of what he had meant by *'This'*.

Was it simply friendship that he was talking about or was it more?

Few of my classmates had warned me to pull my horses as they believed he was going around with someone from his batch. I had myself seen him a few times with a girl – too short for him and too quiet for my understanding. But my analysis of their body language when they were together had me reassured – to put it simply, they looked too dull together.

Well, I was in no hurry to implore into personal matters as at the moment. I was more than happy on the road that destiny was taking me.

Everyday had become so special now that I had something more to look forward to. And the excitement that was brimming inside of me had quadrupled knowing that he liked me.

Did he like me?! Of course, he did!

Random phone calls became a habit very soon for us and it wasn't too long before we were talking daily on the phone. It was easy to know that most of the time he did not actually quite have something to call me up for so he would use some pretext or the other to reach me. Initially it would be some official work – collating the names of participants, or discussing an event, taking my opinion on rules and so on. At times I would know it was for real, at times I knew he was faking it and just wanted to talk.

The latter ones were always more special.

He did not want me to spend my phone balance by calling him daily so he was the one who made the calls. Even if I would call, he would reject it and call me back.

"It's my pleasure to call you up – you shouldn't be the one paying for it," he would say in fine chivalry.

I valued his sweet gentleman mannerism. Every evening I would wait for his call. And without fail, my phone would receive it daily. Then one day the call did not come.

I waited patiently for half an hour past our usual time. And half an hour was enough to make me restless.

I called. The bell rang twice and got rejected.

My phone beeped

Busy at the moment, call you back in 15 minutes.

I read the message a tad sad. My precious time was being used up for some other work. We did not talk past dinner as my mother did not like me to be on my phone for too long into the night. With a slightly heavy heart I began the wait, passing my time in flipping the pages of *Grey's Anatomy.*

Fifteen minutes passed. I checked my phone. Nothing.

Twenty minutes. Still nothing.

Thirty minutes.

My patience was being tested now. I decided to have some fun. I sent a message, rather a song; Amitabh Bachchan's famous one from *Sharabi....*

'*...Intehaa ho gayi, intezaar ki... Aayi na kuch khabar, mere yaar ki...*

Ye hume hai yakeen, bewafa woh nahi... Fir wajah kya hui, intezaar ki....'

I laughed a little wicked giggle on my own cheesy antic and hit send. Within a minute, my phone was ringing. It was Him.

"Helllooooooooooo," I sang into the receiver, as melodiously as I could.

"Hey!" His voice always had the same effect on me – deep, soft and rich it tickled something inside my tummy and made me close my eyes.

Each and every time.

"What's this song?" He asked softly.

"Well, you know what it is – the rue of a forlorn lover waiting for his beloved....." I cooed gently.

"Is that who I am? Your beloved?" I caught the apparent humour in his voice.

I played along, my spirits high.

"The song can be used for more purposes, you know.... It's not a rule to use it only in one perspective."

"Hmm, agreed."

And that's how my flirting increased in leaps and bounds. Within a mere span of two weeks, our relation had become free and easy. No more were our talks limited to official stuff. We became more unceremonious – our conversations changed to daily updates about college, professors, gossip, family, friends, likes, dislikes and so on.

Although he was reserved in expressing his feelings, he never seemed to mind my coquetry. He would always take it in good spirit and laugh along, though he never gave wind to the fire. Not that I needed any wind. I was all fire and tempest. Barring the limitations that I had self imposed since adolescence, I was nothing but vociferous in my romantic advances. It was on one such daring occasion, that I almost forth rightly proposed him.

"Hey, I'm in the market. You need something?" All bright and chirpy he almost shouted over the chaos of traffic that I could here in the background.

"Yeah!" I wickedly replied. "Is there a shop for spare parts somewhere in that market?"

"Mmm... There must be one. I'll check it out. What do you need?" he asked, not minutely aware of what was going to follow.

"Well, I've actually lost my heart. Could you get a spare one for me from that shop?" I casually spoke into the phone.

After several minutes of sweet silence, he could finally manage to speak up.

"You're crazy...." Softly he whispered.

With all the truth and dare in my heart, I smiled and closed my eyes in the conviction of my reply...

'Only for you.'

Week 3

While staying connected on the phone became a habit, the chances of sighting him had now become really low.

Partially because of the packed schedules that we had – lectures, lab work, pre-clinical work – everything was too tight to manage and he was busier, considering he was in the third year and juggling all clinical subjects. Partially because of his dear committee – Raaghav was in love with his work. Dedicated, disciplined, sincere, committed to getting things done – I was in awe of his diligence. But it was his same resolve to work, that kept him busier than bees. I secretly tried getting some snaps in my phone – couldn't be too subtle though!

"What a beautiful view this is!" I faked dramatically, referring to the ruins beside our college when in actuality I was trying to capture him crossing across.

Yet another opportunity came to my advantage when one free period we were all whiling away time in the canteen and in strode none other than Mr Precious. While he ordered, I leisurely snapped away as many pictures of his gorgeous face that I could, and as sophisticatedly as I could manage. The instant that he was out, my friends had me cornered. I was the butt of all jokes these days. And not in the least was I offended; rather I was basking in all the pleasure that my heart seemed to be getting by my name being linked to His.

I was on cloud nine!

Amidst all the chattering, I ordered a coffee and a sandwich realizing how hungry I was as I had left home on an empty stomach. Comments zipped past me like arrows piercing my wounded heart and I relished the bitter sweet pain of being madly in love.

"You're so lost in love, that you've lost all your senses," said Kunal.

I winked across the table.

"The plight of a soul when the heart is in pain," I laughed and pretended to be in severe pain, holding my hand over my heart.

As everyone burst out laughing, I couldn't feign the act any longer. Rolling over in a fit of giggles I accidently tipped over my stool!

Kriti somehow managed to hold me in mid-air and steadied me back.

"You'll break your head before you break your heart, darling," cooed someone on the table.

Some of my friends laughed and I couldn't help but smirk at it myself. This reference of Raaghav being with someone else and simply toying with me had come up quite often. But what was difficult for me to understand was far bigger – my absolute disregard for this apparently big fact. It just did not register as a potential concern for me.

I wondered why.

Our relation was like a patient suffering from Split Personality Disorder, a medical condition in which the personality becomes dissociated into two or more distinct parts, each of which becomes dominant and controls behaviour from time to time to the exclusion of the other part.

To put it simply, it's a person acting like two different individuals, wherein one personality is completely unaware of the existence of the other. This is how we were – in college, one relationship and on the phone, another.

Somehow, there had been this unspoken mutual understanding between us that all our flirtations, no matter how light headed, were reserved for our talks over the phone – never for college.

I had never questioned him on this choice of his. To be honest my heart knew the truth, without him saying it aloud. He had gotten himself into some complicated relationship with little Miss Mute for reasons even he did not understand, and now he felt obliged to stick with her.

It hardly mattered to me. After all, they were just walking to and from the gate to the lecture theatre every day – one look at the monotony in their daily gait together and one could stamp it that there was nothing between them.

No spark, no charm, no fun.

And then I had entered his life, for better or worse, putting him into a dilemma, of sorts.

I had known guys who would leave their partners in a minute if I would have beckoned them, but Raaghav was just so different. He was a deep thinker – kind of archaic in his philosophy, of this I was sure. But for reasons beyond my comprehension, I wasn't in the least perturbed rather I felt a certain attraction to this quality of his.

Maybe things progressed because of the spice that the situation added – a guy being pursued like crazy by a girl. That surely wasn't too common a pattern around.

Maybe it was because I felt free and not threatened by overbearing romantic flirtations? I had developed a certain detest against them, and not having to receive the same from Raaghav was refreshing.

Maybe his laidback nature attracted me more to him?

He wanted to keep our candid relation a secret in college, and I was happy to oblige. It really did not matter that I could not share my happiness with others.

What mattered was having him in my life. I'd do anything for him – at least so, for the moment.

Week 4

The comperes for the evening did not take too long to start and very soon enough the entries for Mr and Ms Fresher were being called on stage.

Raaghav kept to the sidelines of the stage mostly bent over his file. An occasional smile would cross his face on a funny remark by the jury or when he paused to see an interesting act by a candidate. Along the course of time, I eventually got carried away by the fun of the competition and soon enough the next person to be called out was me. Having waited for this moment since the past week I was ready to go!

I walked down the aisle towards the stage as the crowd clapped for me. I could hear a couple of whistles and hoots. I had dressed in a pair of black jeans and my favourite black shirt – I loved the way it hugged all my curves. Although I was wearing my bright pink overcoat because of the cold, the reaction of the crowd as I walked upon the stage was enough proof of me looking hot! But my looks were not the only thing that was going to get me my prize. I had to be the best in the rounds that lay ahead of me, and I was ready to strike!

Walking confidently towards the podium I took the mike off its stand and pulled it with myself towards the very centre of the stage. I smiled at the jury, wished the audience and introduced myself with flare and poise. I kept it brief as we were allowed only a minute for this part and over time meant negative marking.

I was confident of my oratory skills and I was rewarded by a generous applause.

I smiled across the hall, making sure to check out the response from Dr Green Eyes. Apparently, his papers were more interesting to him than I.

As the applause subsided, the mike was passed to the jury. Now came the actual part of the competition. One professor from the jury took the mike and peering over his spectacles, looked at me and smiled.

"So, what are your hobbies?"

Ah, simple question!

"Well I have a lot of hobbies, Sir! I like to keep myself busy – I love to read, I like gardening and often I cycle whenever I'm free. If I'm not in the mood of any of these, then I love to sleep! It's one of my favourite hobbies!"

The crowd burst out laughing as did the members of the jury. My judge was quick to respond to my answer.

"All right, great then! Your task today is to show us ten different sleeping poses right now."

Laughter scattered across the hall.

"Absolutely Sir! That won't be difficult at all."

I smiled as I walked back to the stage and fixed back the mike onto its handle.

"Here we go," I announced. Clasping both my hands together as in a Namaste, I bent them side wards and placed my left cheek over them – "Pose number 1."

Crossing arms over one another in front of me, I placed them over the podium and propped my chin over the centre, closing my eyes – "Pose number 2."

Then in the same position, I ducked my head under my crossed over arms and shouted from beneath my arm caves – "Pose number 3."

There were some claps from the audience that had me motivated further. I straightened up and propped one elbow over the podium, resting my right cheek in the cup of my hand – "Pose number 4."

My mind was working faster now. I had to think out of the out of the box. Surely, this round was to test presence of mind and not intellect – I took my chances! Walking to the side of the podium and turned to face it from the side and leaned forward resting my head over it while my arms dangled loosely in front – "Number 5."

The audience let out a loud laughter and there was a considerable applause! I stood up and leaning against the side of the podium, sprawled out my arm across its top, resting my neck on my elbow, my face turned sideways – "Number 6."

Keeping hold of my stance, I turned my back completely towards the podium and leaned with all my weight onto to it. I crossed my arms and looking down I covered my face with my left hand – gangster style – "Number 7."

Three more to go I thought to myself... I was running out of ideas.

Ahhh, the simplest one! I stood straight and simple let my hands fall beside me, my head drooping to one side, my mouth slightly open as if I was fast asleep – "Number 8."

I crooned as if speaking in a dream. The crowd including the jury was in fits of laughter by this time and I was thoroughly enjoying it. And the last two poses came to me smoothly. With one quick move, I jumped off the stage – barely two feet in height. I sat down near the base of the podium and leaned onto it, resting myself comfortably, closing my eyes I shouted – "Number 9!"

And the final one I thought to myself – I twisted my back towards the podium, and lifted my legs back onto the stage. Without getting up, I extended my legs and crossed one foot over the other, crossed my arms, lay back my head against the podium and for the final time, closed my eyes. Gladly I shouted out, rather announced dramatically – "And that is Pose Number 10!"

Melodrama ran in my blood and the crowd burst out in a thunderous applause! In a jiffy, I got up to my feet and jumped back onto the stage, beaming before the audience. The judges were applauding too and they did look pleased with my performance. I bowed before the audience graciously accepting their generous handclapping.

"Very well done, Miss."

The mike had been taken by another faculty and one look at him and I knew this one was going to ask me my question. He was the one who had been putting up the trickiest questions that evening.

"Thank you Sir!" I smiled.

"Now time for a question," He paused, and threw a dashing smile at me. No wonder so many girls in college had a crush on him! As the word crush fleeted across my mind, I was suddenly reminded that my very own crush – Dr Green Eyes must have seen my erratic sleeping poses, but at the moment I did not dare to break eye contact with my judge. Simply assuming him to be there near the corner of the stage, I waited for my question.

"If you had a chance to go out on a date with someone, whom would that person be?"

For a moment I thought I had heard the question wrong!

Before I could even absorb it, my wild friends in the audience, started shouting from the back of the room.

"Say it! Say it!"

"Today is your chance!"

"Say it!"

I loved my friends! I grinned out to them and the judges looked back to see who was shouting. The crowd was whispering incoherently and a few more students chipped in with the shouts.

The lecturer who had asked me the question looked absolutely amused and as he turned to face me I caught him laughing. I decided to play along.

"Sir, does it have to be someone from this room only?"

"Yes! Yes! Yes!" My friends had gone crazy!

I chuckled out loud and waited for Sir's answer, who had raised his hand attempting to quiet down the crowd. Leaning forward he looked straight into my eyes,

"*Now*, it has to be from this room!"

As he put down his mike, asserting that the question was complete, the audience responded with whoops and hollers and the tempo rose as my name was being cheered! My grin couldn't have been any bigger and I felt myself blushing as Raaghav's face flashed across my mind. I turned towards the right side of the stage just managing to see a figure walk right out of the hall!

It did not even take me a millisecond to be sure who had left.

It had to be Him – the split personality president, Dr Green Eyes.

Amidst the perked up cheering of the audience, I looked down and smiled – I wasn't going to take your name, baby. Perfectly sure of myself I gave my answer.

"I would love to take a name from this room, but there are so many in this room who would want to go on a date with *me*!" I tinkered, the crowd hooting and cheering!

"So I'd rather take a name *outside* of this room."

The audience had approved my answer and the lecturer couldn't help but appreciate along with them.

"Smart answer!" he nodded, signalling me to go on.

"If given a chance to go out on a date, I would love to go out with Leonardo DiCaprio."

Another female faculty in the jury asked for the mike.

"But Leonardo doesn't seem to be a very stable option considering the rumours surrounding his rehab from drug abuse," she jeered.

"As you yourself are saying they are rumours, it shall not be wise to pay heed to them. But even if he is on drugs I can assure you that if I spend an hour with him I'll convince him out of it completely." Brimming with assertiveness, I literally threw the answer in her face.

The crowd burst into a booming applause and the jury looked satisfied. I smiled joyfully. I had done well.

The handsome lecturer who had asked me the question of the evening took the mike from her hand and laughingly concluded.

"Well done, Miss. Thank you!"

I smiled back and graciously bent in response.

Looking across the hall I thanked the audience, and surrounded by claps and cheers, headed back to my friends who engulfed me in a group hug.

"You were amazing!"

"What a performance!"

As I high-fived and hugged them back, settling into my space I turned back hoping to see Raaghav back in the room. But he was nowhere to be seen.

I joined my friends in cheering for the next participant and it didn't take too long for the competition to come to a close.

I walked out of the room surrounded mostly by my friends, but I was amused as people from everywhere were coming up to congratulate me, appreciating my performance, wishing me luck and hoping that I win the title.

And there amidst a crowd of students – tall, lean and lost in his work was my Angel. He was now dressed in a dark grey suit with a lighter grey shirt and looked even more dashing than I had ever imagined. My heart melted at the very sight of him. Dazed again by the sheer sexiness of his height, I walked slowly towards the stage – smitten and completely owned.

The lawn was all ready and set up for the show – an evening of the Annual Day celebrations which would culminate with the announcement of Mr and Ms Fresher. With one last look at busy Raaghav behind the stage, I headed to the girls hostel at the back of the stage to get ready for the fashion show. I was depicting an Indian lady from the 80s – traditional saree, deep cut blouse, high bun, kohled up eyes and the stuff.

It didn't take me too long to get ready and I wasn't eager to waste precious time that could be utilized in ogling at Dr Green Eyes. Catching the slightest opportunity I sneaked out of the room and cautiously made my way backstage. Just as I turned around the corner of the hall I bumped straight into a tall figure of heavenly smelling cologne. As I managed to retain balance in my saree, two firm arms firmly grasped me by my shoulders and steadied me up.

The lighting was dim but the light of my hope shone brilliantly and as if by the hint of some super power I just knew who I had landed into – it was *Raaghav*. His lips were slightly parted and he seemed to be in a state of daze. He took a good couple of minutes gazing upon me before he let go.

"You, Miss Confidence, are so beautiful." He sighed satisfactorily. "May I, with your permission, give a personal touch?"

I could already feel myself becoming more beautiful under his gaze. You don't know the kind of personal touches you have on me, baby, I thought shyly and gently nodded.

From the top pocket of his coat he took out a Parker pen. Slowly he inched closer to me, his eyes fixed upon mine. His emerald gems were brilliantly lit and looked more verdant than ever.

As he moved in, I stretched my neck backwards to follow his face towering upon me. He was the perfect height! Just as I had always imagined leaning for a kiss – he was it!

He smiled as if he could read my thoughts and I could feel the heat from my blushing cheeks. Gently, he used the clip of his pen like a hair pin and tugged out a light flick from the left side of my head. Softly he rolled the little tuft of hair over his finger and then let it fall loose on my cheek.

"There!" He stepped back admiring his artwork, and with a fleeting glance at my lips he darted away, leaving me numb with bliss.

Our moment was too short to seep into my senses completely and I would have thought it to be imaginary had it not been for the physical presence of the flick hugging my cheek. My heart was doing its joyous moment gig.

But I didn't get too much time on my cloud as my fellow performers rushed around me.

It was our turn on the stage.

I laughed at the total weird steps that Kriti was throwing at me to mimic.

Our fashion show had been a total success and the grand event had culminated fantastically for me – after all I had been crowned Ms Fresher by none other than Mr President himself. Of course, it was technically Principal Ma'am who had put on my sash, but it was Raaghav who had given it to her in the first place.

The celebration in my gang of friends was huge as the title of Mr Fresher had also been bagged by none other than Kunal. The group had double the reason to celebrate. Without wasting time, we had quickly changed back into our comfy casuals, hitting the dance floor to enjoy the minutes we had on hand, before dinner was served. I stepped aside a little from the dance floor as the mobile in my jeans pocket vibrated.

Stop dancing.

I stared at the message, completely confused by what it actually meant. Why on earth was Raaghav asking me to stop dancing?

I looked up from my phone into the scattered crowd of people sitting in the seats. Most of the seats were vacant with just a few students here and there. In no time, I found him sitting in the third row from the front. There were a couple of other guys and girls sitting around him merrily chatting and laughing away. But he seemed to be absorbed in his own thoughts.

But why had he asked me stop dancing? Quickly I typed in a simple *Why?!*

I couldn't even keep back my phone as almost instantly it was beeping again.

Because what you're doing is not dancing

I stared at the reply for a complete minute.

Are you kidding me?! He didn't even have the guts to come on the dance floor but comment he could from the side lanes!

Ahan? If you're such an expert then why don't you come on the floor and teach me?

I hit 'send' and went back to my dancing without even turning back to look at his reaction. Not in the least, did I expect him to come up. That much I knew him by now. I continued to dance, my mind fully aware to any vibration that my phone might give. A good couple of minutes passed away and my grey cells started worrying too soon.

Why wasn't there any reply from him till now? Surely, he couldn't be typing in such a long message. Had I offended him? I turned to face the seats.

Lo and behold... He wasn't there!

Almost frantically I tried to scan the ground, amidst all the frenzied dancing people around me, when suddenly the lights went off. Some wire must have tripped off in all that wind. It had become pretty dark and not wishing to get myself squished on the crowded dance floor, I started to walk toward the seats. But just as I stepped down the floor, my arm was grasped firmly but softly by a hand. Startled I turned in surprise to face the attacker.

Only to meet those green eyes I had been searching for.

In the midst of all the darkness I could barely see him crossing one long finger over his lips, gesturing me to remain silent.

I smiled and nodded.

"Come with me," he whispered, holding out his hand.

And without a minute's hesitation I put mine in his. It was a wonder how comfortable he made me feel. My trust in him was strong without reasoning. He walked me towards the end of the dance floor, and I presumed that he had most probably come in response to my last message and we would be dancing together.

But we kept walking right past the dance floor and towards the hostel lobby where all the preparations before the function had been going on. We crossed behind the stage, across the lobby platform and reached the hostel entrance. It seemed to be pretty dark inside and just as we reached the gates, he turned and looking towards the dance floor into what seemed an apparently dark wall to me, nodded towards someone.

As if on his command, suddenly all the lights came back! I was impressed. He had the lights go out to steal me out of the crowd! He turned to my smiling face and smiled as he looked at me.

"You can feel comfortable now that the lights are back."

My smile widened as I turned naughty.

"I was so even without the lights."

He arched one eyebrow and gave a lop sided smile.

And I caught a naughty sparkle in his eyes. Or was it just magical glitter? Well, whatever it was, my stomach butterflies had returned from the forest.

As we reached the very last room, he placed one hand on the door handle and paused. Looking deep into my eyes he stood there as if waiting for me to say something. Not even the tiniest corner of my heart suspected this man here of anything wrong and I just stood there staring into his eyes, ready for whatever spectacle he was going to show me behind the door.

"Do you trust me?" he asked his voice soft and gentle as if imploring my feelings for Him.

Here I was with him, standing at the end of the most isolated corridor in the college, about to enter a room with no idea of what was going to happen next, and he was asking me whether I trusted him?!

Seriously?! That was the sweetest thing a man could do and I flashed back a smile that lit up his eyes. I answered, completely honest and without any hesitation,

"Between your heart and mine, there is a special bridge... That I'd cross with eyes closed and no knowledge... "

He smiled that big ear to ear grin and I grinned back.

He opened the door and guided me in. I anticipated seeing something magnificent as the surprise that had been built up was tremendous. But to my confusion, I was left standing in an empty room!

As he switched on just one corner light, my eyes travelled around.

A couple of benches were pushed up against the far wall. A solitary lamp was standing on my left side corner of the room. There was a mirror on the right wall and a table right next to it. Besides this, the room was all empty except for a lot of sparkle and glitter covering the floor in random places, but mostly in front of the mirror.

I turned to find him a little engrossed in his phone and assuming it to be something urgent, I took the opportunity to walk up to the table and explore.

On the table, was a magician hat, lots of ribbons, a make-up box, colourful feathers, a few trays of glitter and sparkle, a bottle of ice spray, lots of markers, coloured tapes and a thick pile of what seemed like satin dress material.

"This must have been the room where the dance performers for today's function dressed up!" I exclaimed as it struck me!

"Precisely! You seem to be quite intelligent."

Looking up through the mirror right in front of me, I found him gazing at me. Poised perfectly, leaning on the door with one leg crossed over the other, hands in his pocket.

Gosh! He looked so sexy!

I turned to face him and tried to read his face. I surely got that last comment. I raised an eyebrow, questioning what was going on and he got it completely.

"What you were doing outside, you like to call dancing. I beg to differ."

He paused and tilting his head just slightly as if thinking about something, he completed his statement, "And I'd like to show you what it really is to *dance*."

This. Was. Unbelievable.

"And I have your complete trust?" he implored again.

You can stop worrying about that, baby. I thought in my head.

I reassured him by gently nodding in the affirmative.

He stood straight, talking his hands out his pockets and as if in deliberate slow motion flashed a naughty smile. Turning towards the door he bolted it from the inside.

My heart stopped.

He turned slowly, stopping to face me. Looking at me for just a second he flicked the screen of his phone and the room was filled with a sweet, soft melody. Smiling to the rhythm that was filling up the room, he walked over to where I was standing near the table.

Surprises did not end, as he simple walked past me to the end of the table and picked up a red satin sheet from the top of the table. I turned to face him and in a swift delicate motion he twirled the sheet over my head, bringing it forward from both sides of my back. As a natural response I lifted my arms slightly so that he could easily pull forward his hands and as he did I realized it to actually be a wrap on skirt. Smoothly he crossed the two ends over, right below my navel. Very gently, he turned me towards the opposite wall of the room. I now stood facing the bright light on the corner of the room that blinded me to his face and all I could make out was a silhouette.

Crossing one hand over my head, he moved behind me and for the first time he made contact. I could feel a jitter all through my spine as his hands sat flat across my stomach, caressing out the satin creases. And then slowly, as if deliberate on purpose, he gently glided his hands across my waist on both sides and all the way to the back where he quickly tied a knot to the skirt.

Slowly I opened my eyes, adjusting to the bright light and the picture before me caught my breath.

The mirror was right before us and the satin skirt that he had just tied me into bedazzled elegantly. As I gazed into the mirror following the skirt from my feet towards my waist, I saw his hands gently there. I smiled and glanced up into the mirror to meet the green eyes staring into mine.

We stood there for a moment, and then he moved towards the other side of my frame in the mirror. Without even turning towards the table, he picked up something and my eyes drifted towards his right hand. His left hand still on my waist, he had picked up a tall black hat with the other.

I turned to face him and he let go off me, taking a step backwards. With all the chivalry in the world, putting out his hand he bowed over slightly and looking straight into my eyes he softly asked, "Dance with me?"

I smiled and gently placed my hand in his. With the most stylish sweep I had ever seen, he double flipped the hat onto his arm first and then onto his head, where it landed perfectly. Nodding ever so slightly at me, he pulled me closer.

Placing my hand over his shoulder, he gently took my other hand and started to sway to the rhythm. I could feel his strong shoulder muscle under my hand and the warmth of his hand cupping my waist. He was perfectly taller than me, just the way I had always imagined my guy. But this person holding me so delicately right now was no guy – he was a man.

He was *the* perfect man.

"Is everything okay?" he asked softly, his voice loaded with concern. His sensitivity amused me and I couldn't help but smile.

"Yeah, everything's perfect... Just that I don't know how to dance!"

My meek and honest response must have relieved him of his doubts, and the naughty smile was back on his sculpted face.

"Says who?" he said, flipping off his hat with a flick of his finger.

And without a second's delay he firmly pushed me away! I thought I would fall had I not known that he was still holding onto my hands. He gently let go of one, twirling me around with the other and then letting go off both. As if by magic, I kept twirling on my own and just when I thought I was about to tip over, I was grasped by my waist and turned over. As I half stood half fell back over his arm, my hands dangling on both sides, he gently got hold of my hair clip and freed my tresses. Pulling me back to my feet, he helped me stand up and maintained a good distance but did not let me go. I could feel his eyes all over me, as if the warmth of his jewels was touching me wherever his eyes travelled. First they comfortably dived into mine, leisurely travelling over to my nose, then to my dangling earrings.

"Dance is about connection," he cooed. "And I think we have one between us."

We flowed with the music, the satin skirt shimmering along in sync with the beats with my open hair rippling everywhere in a frenzy of their own – I was but a mere puppet in his hands. A happy one, no doubt! And then in the moment of moments, he strongly pulled me over to him. Both hands on either side of my waist he picked me up and placed my feet over his. My hands were resting on his shoulders, but the proximity was now too much to restrain from. I curled over my arms around his neck leaning further into his body.

I gazed into his eyes as he gazed back into mine, slowly moving to the music. He carried me across the room, gently swaying.

As we reached the table, my back towards it, he stopped. His eyes were once again all over my face and I moved my fingers into his hair – soft like feathers.

"Have I ever told you how beautiful you are?"

I smiled and nodded. He put me down on my feet, walked slowly to my side and once again I was revealed to my image in the mirror across the room. I saw him pick up something in the reflection before he turned back to stand beside me, one hand again at the back of my waist. Looking at me in the mirror he stretched his hand before the fan standing on to the right of us.

"Well, you're not just beautiful."

Lo and behold! There was glittering sparkle all around me and how charming it looked in the mirror.

"You're magic!"

We stood in what seemed to me like an illusion, lost in our fairy land, just gazing into our reflection till the music got over. Silence filled the room and I could hear my breath. But his breath I could *feel* on the nape of my neck and suddenly I felt myself go warm and mushy. I could see myself blush in the mirror as he softly whispered into my ear.

"And this is how I like to dance."

As I saw his reflection walk away I turned to face him. Reaching the door, he pocketed his silent phone and unbolted the door. With one quick glance towards me he smiled his charming best, nodded and left. I was left standing alone in the room. The beating of my heart was so loud it could have burst out, literally!

All around me was glitter and towards the corner of the room was the hat – *his* hat. I walked across to the hat, gently picking it up and dusting away the glitter that it now adorned. It was a night to remember, so a souvenir was worth it.

"You're a lucky hat!" I mumbled to it.

I had gone totally crazy after all, so what was the big deal in talking to a hat. Holding the hat close to my heart, as if it were a baby, I closed my eyes to relive the moments that had just gone by. Dancing in Raaghav's arms, completely lost to the world around me, exhilarated by the joy of being in love.

"Ira!"

My sweet reverie was interrupted when I heard my name being called out. It must be Kriti who must have by now noticed my absence. I did not want to open my eyes and go back into the moment of reality waiting for me outside the door. And while I was contemplating whether to reply to her shouts or not, I suddenly felt someone jerking my arm!

"Ira! Wake up! You'll get late for college!"

Whoa! Late for college?! I am already in college! What was happening?!

In utter bewilderment, I opened my eyes, only to shut them back again as the sunshine blinded me across the window. I opened my eyes again and blinked several times, before coming to the realization. It had been a dream!

I was lying on my bed, practically clinging to my pillow. What a dream it had been!

As the sweet scenes from my dream flashed across my mind, I halted at the moment when he had me on his feet and we had held on to each other. His perfectly carved face adorned with an adorable smile, his emeralds as sparkling as ever, drowning me into the depths of an enchanting abyss and in an instant I was absolutely sure – I was in love.

I was totally, madly, deeply and irrevocably in love with Raaghav.

As I reluctantly got up and prepared myself for the day ahead, my mind wandered away to the *actual* happenings of the day before – Fresher's Day.

I glanced across the room to see my latest achievement – The Ms Fresher tiara and sash that hung elegantly over my room door and the tall hat that Raaghav had been toying around with back stage. I had stolen it when no one was looking.

My dream had been such a mix up of the realities and desires – a feisty concoction, to say the least.

The reality had not been all bland either. Less intoxicating maybe, but surely refreshing. I had danced away to my heart's desire with my gang of crazy friends. My joy of being crowned Ms Fresher had held my spirits high and although a little corner of my heart was always in search for him, most of my consciousness had managed to have a great time.

The dinner had gotten quite late and I was glad I did not have to go back home alone. Settled into the back seat of Kriti's car, reliving the sweet moments of the day, I did not realize how time had flown by and the long distance from college to home was covered quickly.

I had already messaged Mum that I would get late and she need not worry as Kriti would be dropping me. As I searched for the hidden key outside the entrance door, I could feel my phone vibrating. I rushed to my room. There was no guessing who was calling at this hour.

It had to be Him – Dr Green Eyes.

I flicked my phone open and gently whispered into the speaker.

"Hi!"

"Hey!" His warm voice filled in the silence of the night. He wasn't whispering. But was surely talking a tad softer than usual.

"Reached home safely?"

"Yeah, just a minute ago." I smiled.

"Someone was supposed to message me," he sang out in a song.

"I was about to in a second..." I was trying as best as I could manage to be coherent through whispering into the speaker. This was new for me. I had never before talked to someone so late at night, and that someone being a guy was even more threatening if my parents would get to know about it. My heart was beating fast – out of fear or out of the excitement of doing something forbidden, I was yet to decide.

"So, Ms Fresher, how do you feel?"

Ah! He hadn't simply called up to make sure I had reached home safely. He was in the mood to talk. I was ever ready.

"Well...." I toyed with the word that I wanted to use. "I'm feeling alone. Top of the world but alone," I summed it up. It was honest to much of an extent. It had been a big day yet the privilege of having him solely for me had been miniscule.

"Oh, but you're not alone, are you?" he asked in the honey coated voice of his that had me drooling.

"Not now..." I whispered back, tentatively seductive.

"Hmm...." He was contemplating something. "I like the way you're talking...." He was whispering now and what an instant effect it had on me! My stomach had completely curled up into knots. My cheeks were flushing and my breathing had turned shallow.

"I think it's a good idea if both of us talk in whispers..." He was deliberately speaking slower, more musically than normal and it was just too tempting for me.

"This could be potentially dangerous for us," I whispered into the phone.

"Mm-hmm..." His voice was suggestive though back to normal. I could vaguely hear someone in the background.

"Yes, I'll take it tomorrow," he answered, maybe to the voice in the room. So that is why he was back to normal.

"Ya, so where were we?" He was back on the phone.

"Well, I'm here in my house and you are there in yours. So... we're actually not *we*... Just you and me." It was my turn to play.

"Hmmm..."

Suddenly I remembered I had to talk to him about his walking out of the Fresher's when I was on stage.

"Why did you walk out of the Fresher's when I was asked about whom I would like to date?"

He took his time to answer. I waited patiently.

"Well... I was kind of scared..."

"Scared, that I'll take your name?"

He had gone too quiet. I didn't need to put him through this. I was completely aware of his unsaid fears and I took pride in understanding them.

"You do trust me, Raaghav?" I asked softly. "I'd never do something to make you feel uncomfortable," I said softly.

"I know. I trust you. It's just that you're friends started shouting and then the crowd pitched in. I didn't know what to do. You love the limelight, Ira. You're so much at ease at being the centre of attraction in a room filled with more than a hundred people. It's fantastic! I mean... I envy it... But me, I'm a very reserved kind of a person... I was shy in school... I had a lot of difficulty making friends... Even today in college, I don't have too many."

Raaghav had never bared his heart to me the way he was doing today. I was deeply touched. Suddenly I was feeling all protective about him.

"Joining the college committee and giving my best is an attempt to be a part of a big group – to prove my worth, to be appreciated and known for... To be someone who is... Not alone..." His voice faded.

"You're not alone..." I whispered gently into the phone.

The trust that he put in me was evident and I valued it deeply.

"I know..." he whispered back.

Oh, how I wanted to hug him!

"You know, you're one fantastic leader." I tried lifting his spirits. "I was the school Head Girl and I know the bulk of responsibilities and pressures that come along with the post. You do a great job! Today's event was beyond fantastic – all thanks to your perfect management." I enthusiastically tried to pep him up. And it worked! He laughed softly on the other side.

"Of all the people in college, you are the most biased to appreciate me!" He was back in his usual happy mood. "There were a lot of glitches in today's program."

"Really?! See you managed those glitches so well, that I being an audience, as well as a participant, did not feel them at all!"

"That's because you're always so lost..." He mocked.

"Well, I like being lost," I stated with conviction. "The real world is sometimes too boring and dull, but in my dreams and imagination, I can lose myself in candy clouds and chocolate trees... I can meet creatures from alien lands or become an alien myself... I can run away from someone I dislike, and get close to someone I do like..."

"Hmmmm... So, who do you want to get close to?" he asked, back to whispering. I knew he was smiling.

"Oh, that I told the entire college today... Leonardo DiCaprio!" I answered triumphantly as his laughter filled my ears.

"That was a damn good performance that you gave! Too good! There was no doubt you wouldn't win!"

He had liked my performance and was praising it. I was beaming with delight! And as we talked into the morning our casual friendship evolved into something else. Something I had never felt before.

In the realm of that one night I was opened to a new side of my fondness for him and this new window was beautifully enchanting.

As he dozed off on the phone somewhere close to five, I was hypnotized by the rhythmic sounds of his breathing.

He felt so close, as if sleeping just beside me.

So close, so warm, so sexy.

With ravishing thoughts beyond the grasp of words, I too fell into a deeply satisfying sleep. My heart and mind in peace with the decision that had been made.

My feelings were ready to progress.

The news was a huge opportunity for me! The college photographer had taken good shots of the entire program and we were allowed to buy the ones we liked at a nominal charge.

I, along with Kriti and Kunal, had rushed to the Administration Department minutes after the announcement, laughing wickedly over my plan. Given Raaghav's involvement in the function, I was sure there would be a good number of pictures which would have captured him. And it was my chance to steal away a few. Well, purchase actually. I would be paying for them, after all.

We were the first ones to reach the office as was apparent from the collection of snaps – none of them had been taken. Glancing through, my heart overflowed with joy. My guess turned out to be right!

Full HD coloured photographs of Raaghav captured in different moments from the Annual Day – what a feast to the eyes! Almost every three to four pages was one snap that would make my heart beat faster!

As planned, Kriti and Kunal started an irrelevant conversation with the administrative officer. We thought it would be safer if no one knew what I was going to do. I pretended to scan though the album searching for my snaps. As soon as the two of them managed to distract the officer away to the forms section, I quickly removed all six snaps that had Raaghav in the frame. Just so that his snaps could be hidden from the administrator's as well as other prying eyes, I took out two of mine. Placing one on top of the collection of six and one below, I sandwiched his snaps carefully.

"I'm done!" I called out aloud, to which the administrator came back running in a hurry. Holding the snaps down on the table, I gently counted them before him, simply picking up a corner so as to keep them hidden.

"...five, six, seven and eight." I announced, almost triumphantly!

Kriti and Karan had bugged him well and it was easy to judge that he simply wanted us be gone! I winked to them standing behind him to assure them of the success of our plan, as he calculated my due charges for the eight snaps.

My attempts at capturing him in the insignificant camera of my phone had been quite futile, though I had not given up. Whatever blurred and hazy images of him I had managed to get, I had never deleted a single one of them. And the latter half of most of my evenings would be spent staring at the sub optimal snaps.

But these, full HD completely digital proper pictures, these were like diamonds for me! Now I could see him whenever I wanted to. Also, for the first time, I now had a decent chance of showing his face at home.

Ravi had already started teasing me about the guy with whom I was always on phone. I loved my little brother deeply and I was thrilled at the thought of showing him the much hyped over green eyed face!

As far as Mom was concerned, well I did keep mentioning about the great college President and his fantastic management from time to time. We had also once randomly talked about his height, for what reason, I could not remember now. Somehow, the reactions from Mom had been quite different of late. I had not been getting too many positive re-enforcements in opening my heart to her.

I disembarked from my van and ran up the stairs. My spirits were too high to be contained and as I barged into my house, I dived straight into Ravi's room.

"There's something I have to show you!" I panted excitedly as I searched my bag.

He had been reading but was glad to see me. Putting down his book, he rubbed his eyes in an attempt to awaken himself from his study slumber.

"Ta da!" I put down out the envelope before him as if it were an act of magic.

A look of confusion spread across his face, he picked up the envelope and tried to ascertain its weight.

"What's this?" he asked.

"Ha ha!" I exclaimed, "Mr Green Eyes! On digital photographic paper!"

His eyes widened in delight as he realized the contents of the envelope and within seconds he had the snaps out on his table.

"Wow! He is tall yaar, Deedee! Tall, thin and.... sexy!" He smiled, looking at me naughtily.

I blushed! Brimming with joy, I hugged my sweet little brother tightly and quickly collected my gems from his table.

"Now, Mom's turn!"

"I'll come too!" he chirped excitedly.

Shutting his book, he jumped out of his chair and out went the both of us searching for Mom. She was in her room, chopping some vegetables. I stopped Ravi midway before we reached her and quietly whispered in his ear.

"Pretend you haven't seen the snaps."

"Yeah, she might get hurt that you showed them to me before her," he added, bro-fisting me.

Casually, I walked into her room while Ravi loitered around in the living room.

"Hey, what's up?" I asked.

"Getting stuff ready for dinner," she answered engrossed in her work.

"I wanted to show you something... Rather someone..." I smiled.

She looked up.

"The much talked about..."

Saying so I dropped the snaps out onto the bed

"...here we have, Dr Raaghav Mehra!" I announced proudly!

I was like a little child showing the trophy that I had won for a race in school today. But the enthusiasm did not last long as Mom splashed cold water right over the blazing fire in my heart.

"Oh, he's so skinny! Kind of weird actually..." she rebuked.

"You don't find him smart?!" I blurted out, absolutely taken aback by her icy reaction.

"This?" She pointed the snaps with the knife in her hand, "This is not smart at all."

Just at that very moment, Ravi strolled into the room.

"Hey, what's happening? Oooo... Who's here?" He pretended to be caught by the snaps lying on the bed, so brutally rejected by Mom.

For a minute I thought, she'd answer Ravi's question but she didn't.

"This is Raaghav..." I said turning towards him so that my back was toward Mom.

"Hmm. Your senior, right? The committee President," he pretended to be recollecting from memory, snapping his fingers.

Truly, he was a great actor, just like his expert sister. From the corner of his eyes he looked at Mom. She was back to her veggies with no interest in us, it seemed. Ravi gave me a questioning look.

I shrugged. Going through the snaps he observed them carefully as if seeing them for the first time. "He's smart... isn't he, Mom?"

"Huh!" she retorted without a second's delay. That was enough for me.

"Of course, he's smart! Half the girls of my batch have a crush on him!" I directed my answer towards Mom rather than Ravi.

And not wanting to spoil my moment of celebration, I gathered the snaps from under Ravi's nose and walked out to my room. I didn't care whether Mom approved of his looks or not. I didn't care.

Suddenly, I felt like writing.

In one move I collected my gems and delicately carried them over to the study table. Placing them in one corner, I took out my diary and opened it to a fresh page. My green pen was just where I had left it last time – in the drawer on the top right of the work station. Since the day I had been smitten by these emerald green eyes that lay before me now, I had started making all the entries in my diary in green. Closing my eyes momentarily, I sighed as the lines filled up my heart.

> *Love messes up the heart in ways more than one...*
> *It's senseless, it's crazy and it's so much fun...*
> *You feel like drowning when you are actually rising...*
> *The irony of feelings can be quite surprising...*
> *Love makes you breath deep, it makes you feel alive...*
> *It gives you peace like a night long drive...*
> *The stability of roots is what it brings...*
> *But you fly high, as it also gives you wings...*
> *Safe haven becomes a lover's embrace...*
> *The moon – a reflection of one sweet face...*

Few moments apart and the world starts breaking...
Togetherness – the only relief to heart's aching...
Yet love cannot be understood as a word...
A storm of emotions gently stirred...
The purpose of one's existence is to fall in love...
Grow in love and rise above...

I put down my pen and turned the page.

I picked up each jewel of my precious loot, gazing into the green eyes. Carefully I placed them inside my diary, capturing him in one more place other than my heart. This had been a big feat.

Proudly, I cuddled back into the sheets to indulge in his thoughts.

It was time to dream again.

Things were different now. Though, none of us had overtly expressed our feelings, the status was becoming apparent.

"I think I'm in love," I had once gone forward and put it out.

"Mm hmmm?" He had stopped mid track in his sentence. "And if I may ask, who is the lucky guy?"

"So, you think the one I'd love would be lucky?" I had probed eagerly, making due note that he had pretended not knowing who I was crazy for.

"Of course! You are the perfect girl, Ira. Just like they show it in the movies! You're beautiful *and* sexy... You're intelligent *and* smart... You're funny *and* sensitive... You know how to enjoy life... You can make anyone feel happy just by your presence!" he declared honestly in one breath!

"And you're tall!" he added with genuine awe for my height.

I laughed!

Raaghav generally had this blanket with which he would cover up all his emotions and this blanket of his was always tucked tightly around him. That was probably why I felt so privileged when he would open up to me. Honestly, I had no clue how to react.

"So who is this guy?" he asked again, a ting of playfulness in his voice. He knew me too well to believe that I would flirt with him 24*7 yet fall in love with some other guy. I played along.

"Well... It isn't a guy actually..." I mumbled.

"You mean, it's a girl?!" he shrieked loudly to feign shock, failing miserably at it!

"Thank God, you're becoming a dentist and not an actor! You're pathetic at acting!" I cried out between fits of laughter. He laughed with me. The deep throated laugh that I could listen to all day. It was the sweetest melody for my ears and the smoothest relaxant for my nerves, just like a warm cup of peppermint tea

After laughing to our heart's desire, we both went into silence. Something unsaid was being heard and we both liked it. We both knew our feelings were getting stronger by the day. It was only a matter of time before one of us put it out on the table.

I was struggling hard to refrain myself.

My motive was simple. I did not want to put him into a difficult situation. But my heart was raging a war with my mind. I wanted him.

Softly, he asked again, "So, you're not telling me?"

Oh, I wish I could baby. Only if I could.

How crazy I had become to be loved by you.

How deeply I wanted to be with you... To touch you, hug you, kiss you and make you mine. Only mine.

How I wish!

"I got nothing to hide from you, Raaghav..." I began softy.

"I think... I'm in love... with..." I spread the words with exaggerated pauses, "...doughnuts!" I merrily sang into the phone, covering my feelings with yet another facade.

"Hmmm..." He understood very well what I had done there.

We laughed softly, nevertheless. What the future was holding for the two of us, I could never know.

But the present was the most beautiful gift of my life.

And one that I was eager to unwrap.

⌘

Upon realizing that we had never talked about how he travels to and from college, I decided find out. I could always just simply ask him about it, but that wasn't so much fun as the plan I had in mind. I was a shade of a discoverer. Thankfully, I had cooperative friends and without much difficulty I had them in.

Our classes ended earlier than his and we passed time, chit chatting in the library. Soon enough the hustle bustle across his doors started and the three of us dashed out of our hall, running upstairs to the canteen area. Huffing and puffing we reached the main lawns in front of the canteen. We had to pretend that we hadn't been waiting specially for Raaghav and so Kunal quickly rushed in and bought us three coffees. We dropped onto the grass, took out a couple of registers and began our little act. I sat facing the college building to keep a look out, for when Raaghav would exit. But wouldn't this be too obvious... I wondered.

"Kunal, switch places with me... Quick!" I jumped up and tugged his heavy arm.

"Okay! Okay! You're going to spill my coffee!"

"Kunal! Focus, please!"

Kriti was giggling uncontrollably.

"Now..." I started as I settled into the warm sun, facing the canteen door. "You have to tell us as soon as he comes out of the building, okay?" I stated looking Kunal in the eye.

"And immediately you have to start packing our bags?" I ordered like a commander to Kriti.

"Aye, aye Captain!"

"While the two of you are packing here, I'll go and throw..."

"He's here!" Kunal suddenly interrupted me, trying to speak through gritted teeth.

Raaghav was here! "Who's he with?"

"I think it's Dhruv Sir..."

"Perfect!" I exclaimed. In an instant I jumped up and snatched the coffee cups out of their hands.

"Completely crazy she has become!" I could hear the two of them laughing as I walked towards the canteen.

I was sure Raaghav and his friend would go to the canteen to retrieve their helmets. Dhruv Sir seemed to one of Raaghav's closest friends and he would often leave with him on his bike. Praying for the same to happen today I entered the canteen and turned towards the dustbin just to the right of the door. Above the bin was a window and I managed to peep out of it as I bent over to throw the coffee cups. Raaghav was walking to the left and they were about to reach the canteen door.

My heart beat accelerated. I walked back to the door and paused at the corner of the wall. I scanned around. The canteen was almost empty. I looked down and closed my eyes.

One... two... three. I walked out of the door – banging right into Raaghav!

"Oops!" I feigned in perfect surprise.

Out of the corner of my eye, I noticed Dhruv Sir suppressing a laugh as he walked past us into the canteen.

"Sorry!" I smiled sweetly at Raaghav.

He smiled back knowingly. He was well aware of my frolics by now and he knew the bump had been deliberate. But I was not over with it. He steered slightly to his left in an attempt to enter the canteen. I steered along with him. He then steered a little to his right and I copied suit. He stepped back, all the while smiling, and put out his left hand like a gentleman, "Ladies first."

"Thank you!" I bowed my head ever so slightly and triumphantly walked towards my giggling friends at the end of the park.

"Such a player you are, Ira!" Kunal mocked at me.

"Your second bumping right?!" Kriti winked and I was reminded of the Fresher's Night behind-the-stage moment. That one had actually been by accident. A beautiful accident.

"So, what next?" asked Kunal as we scrambled into his car.

"Now, we leave the college and wait outside near the coconut fellow till they come out on Dhruv Sir's bike."

"Yeah, that's good! Let's have some coconut water."

"Kunal! Focus!" Both Kriti and I shouted together.

"Just joking, just joking!" he laughed throwing his hands up in the air as if accepting defeat. He drove us out of the college gate and positioned the car perfectly across the road. I turned back to see Dhruv Sir's bike exiting the gate – all in perfect timing.

I whispered, "Let them drive a little further and then we start following them, okay?"

"Sure!"

As the bike crossed our car, the three of us ducked to hide our faces.

A minute later, we started our pursuit.

"Okay sweetie!" Kriti crooned pulling the window screen down.

"Thanks a lot guys! You're the best friends one could ever ask for." I leaned in to hug her and fist bumped Kunal.

Glad over another triumph, I merrily ran up the stairs home. Ravi was watching cartoons.

"Hey! I'm home!" I yelled out to him over the excessively loud noise of the TV.

"Hey! Had a good day?" He smiled naughtily and I completely understood where he was going with it.

"One of the best!" I crooned back before heading to my room.

Dropping my bag, I fell onto my bed and gladly did what I loved doing every evening.

Reached home.

I hit send and let the phone fall onto my tummy and started counting.

One, Two, Three...

This had become quite a ritual for the last few days. No longer did we talk at a set time or for a set period time. It was much more now. Our phone connection began when I reached home. For that was the time he felt most comfortable, knowing me to be alone.

Four, Five, Six...

So as soon as I would reach home, I would text him.

Seven, Eight...

And he would call me back in less than ten seconds.

My phone buzzed. I picked it up.

Dr Green Eyes.

Always, less than ten seconds! I smiled and picked up the phone.

"Hey!" I let out a soft voice laced with charm.

I was going to be asked a good number of questions today and I had planned to keep him distracted, with powers of reasoning as well as seasoning.

Reasoning for his mind and seasoning for his heart.

"Hey!" he answered calmly.

"Long day, huh?" I asked genuinely.

"Naaaa... Yours was longer."

Straight to the point. He wasn't in the mood to play around.

"Why did you do it, Ira?"

I tried to read his voice, but he had his blanket up to his nose and I just couldn't penetrate.

"Do what?" I played it difficult.

"You know..." He sighed softly. "Why did you stay back after class? Was it just to catch another glimpse of me? Was it just because you wanted to bump into me? Was it so that you could follow me and Dhruv? What was it?" he exclaimed totally clueless.

"Well..." I began slowly. "It was all of those reasons... I wanted to ogle at you for some more time than usual, I wanted to get close to you by some way or the other and I wanted to know how you get back home... So yeah! All those reasons are correct!"

Silence. This is what I had feared.

This is why I wanted to know his mood before saying anything. I just did not want him to be upset because of me. And this silence thing... I just couldn't deal with on-the-phone silence. And with Raaghav, it was torturous!

"Raaghav, you can be upset or angry with me, but please don't go silent..."

"Ira..." he tried to interrupt.

"I know I might have put you in a little bit of a fix...or..."

"Ira..."

"Or... Maybe a little more of a fix but please don't go quiet... I'm sorry, Raaghav... I'm..."

"Ira... Please stop!" I shut up immediately.

He continued softly, "I'm trying to stop you and you're not listening to me... I did not go quiet out of anger... I was not silent because I had gotten upset, Ira... I was..." he trailed off.

"I was surprised... You said you wanted to get close..." he completed his sentence softly, a pinch of extra emphasis on the word *close*. He had not been expecting such an overt acceptance of emotions from me.

Even though I had just blurted it out, I had meant it completely. I did want to get close to him. I wanted to get much close to him.

I wondered what he was thinking right now.

His response had definitely not been a negative one I analysed. If it would have been negative, he would have used the word 'shock'. But he had said he had been 'surprised'.

This was a good sign. But why wasn't he saying anything more.

"Umm... Yeah, I did say that. And I meant it..." I paused, anticipating a reply but none came. I could hear his soft breathing on the other side.

I had to do it today. I had to talk to him about it, about us. I just had to.

"Raaghav... I don't know how to put this... But I'm going to try anyway. Because I think it's high time I need to say this to you." I began.

"I'm this crazy little girl who joins college, not in the best of her spirits... But I decide to flow with it, living it out like a blast.

And suddenly you're here before me! Just out of my dreams... This simple, soft, mature person... No drama, no frills, no thrills... And the next second I know I have this huge crush on you...! You know it... In fact, what the hell. The entire college knows it! But you never acknowledge it. Because to think of it I've never really said it out clearly... I've played and flirted a lot but never... You know... Never said anything serious... But I also know you see through me and you know what's inside my heart... And I know too what's inside your heart... But you... You've got prior commitments... And that attracts me all the more to you... Coz for me you're this amazing person who is perfect in everything – the perfect leader, the perfect student, the perfect senior and... and the perfect friend... to... whatever her name is..." I hadn't forgotten the little lady's name.

Just didn't want to take it aloud.

"I... I'm sorry, I don't remember her name... But it hardly matters! Coz what I am talking here is about you and me... and her too, kind of... I mean..." I was getting flustered.

This was becoming baffling! Where did she come in from?! What was I trying to say?! Was I even making any sense to him?! I wasn't making any sense to myself!

Aaaaaaaaaaaa......

I turned over and buried my head in my pillow. I didn't know what to say.

"Ira..."

Oh, how I could spend the rest of my life listening to my name being called out in his voice.

"Ira?" he asked with sudden concern.

"Yeah, I'm here," I said finally.

"I'm sorry Raaghav... I shouldn't..."

"Ira..."

"No, I'm really... I didn't mean to be over bearing... I'm so..."

"Ira, I like you!" he interrupted me loudly.

Almost like a reflex, I jerked up in my bed.

"What?! Did you just say that..." I was cut short again.

"Ira... Sshhhh.... Could you now for one moment listen to me, please?"

I obliged, sitting like a statue, not daring to take a breath.

"*Firstly*, her name is Siya. I know you know her name and I'll be happy if taking it aloud wouldn't affect you. *Secondly*, she is not my girlfriend..."

That didn't come as a surprise to me. I knew too well there was nothing between the two of them.

"We became friends in the very beginning of college and for some naive reasons word spread around that we're a couple. It just stuck that way. Whatever it was it never progressed. Rather just became lesser by the day. We've been friends and now we're mostly like batch-mates but we prefer to keep our relationship status to us. *Thirdly*... I am not this perfect person who you think I am. I have my flaws and my imperfections..."

No baby, you need to see through my eyes to know how perfect you are.

"...but you obviously don't see any of those because you are... You are you! That's the fourth thing I want to say and it's the most important for you to know!"

I bit my lower lip.

"You said you're a little crazy girl. No, I disagree. You're not a little crazy! You're this completely mad, silly, full of fun and carefree girl who knows exactly what she wants and doesn't shy away from saying it to the world. You're different, Ira... You're bold! You're daring! You are... You! And I love the way you're you....!"

I sat open mouthed staring at the wall before me.

"Ira, I like you," he whispered into the phone.

I blinked. Was this a dream? I pinched my arm hard.

Ow! No, it definitely was happening for real.

"Ira?" he asked softly.

"Raaghav, I..." Suddenly my smart mouth had nothing to say. My heart beat had accelerated well enough to be heard by the next door neighbour.

"Ira, are you okay?" I could hear his concern.

Okay?! Baby, I am more than okay! No one could have felt any better. But somehow the cat that had caught my tongue was not shooing away.

"I'm fine..." I managed to say. "I'm just... I mean all of this... from you... I.... Raaghav...." I sighed into the phone.

"You've taken me by such a surprise... A very sweet and pretty surprise... And I've fallen for you all over again"

"Yeah, I know..." I knew he was flashing his sexy smile. I could hear it. I closed my eyes wishing he wasn't on the other side of the phone, rather on the other side of the bed.

"And you're right..." I continued dreamily. "I am totally crazy! Absolutely, madly crazy for you..."

I paused.

"I know you like me too, Ira," he hummed into the phone, trying to sum up my emotions.

"No Raaghav. I don't like you..." I replied softly.

"...I love you!"

Admitting the three words I had long wished to put forth before him opened an all new dimension for me. I felt free, as if I had unleashed my heart from the chains it had been hiding behind.

The path that our relation was taking had me increasingly mesmerized. With his covert yet expressive admission of feelings, Raaghav had given me a new reason to hope for more.

He surely had surprised me well with his confessions. Now it was my turn.

"Hey, Kriti!" I shouted out to her over the unusually loud chirping in the class. The lecturer had just left and everyone was gladly packing up to go home. It was a Saturday after all. Half day and the weekend were reasons enough to lift everyone's spirits.

"I got to issue some books and make some photocopies today," I lied as she turned to listen to me. "And I think it's going to take quite some time."

"Oh! But we had all planned to go for lunch today, remember...?" she replied with a sad look.

I had remembered it well enough. But my locus of control was just Raaghav these days. Lunch with friends had to be sacrificed.

"Oh no, I completely forgot!" I feigned shock.

I pretended to think over the situation for a few seconds.

"And I've already asked the librarian to take out all the books for me. He's going to be so pissed off if I don't complete my work today." I put on the saddest expression that I could and flunked back onto my chair.

"Yeah, I know he's so strict...." she agreed. "I think you should go ahead and get your work done. We'll all wait for you in the canteen."

Ooops! I hadn't seen that coming.

Now what was I to do! I needed time to think.

"Okay, great! I'll try and be as quick as I can," I said.

"Cool! I'll go tell the others," she replied.

I high fived her and ran away to the canteen to get my hands on some books for the sake of the drama. I had to convince them to leave. I couldn't tell Kriti about my plan. Raaghav might not like it, knowing that she was involved.

I had to do it alone.

As I took out random books from the ceiling high shelves in the library, my mind raced around the possible options that I had. I couldn't come up with one single idea. Apparently, all that was revolving in my mind was the ecstasy from last night's revelations. The volcanic joy was disrupting all normal thinking capacities.

I was about to settle the books on a table when I saw a figure rush into the library.

"Ira!" yelled out the figure. It was Praveen.

'Sshhhhh!' the librarian retorted vehemently.

I rolled my eyes.

"Sorry, Sir! Sorry!" I could hear him whispering as he headed towards me.

In four quick strides, he was beside me.

"C'mon, let's go," he whispered.

Snatching a few books from my hand he started placing them back on the racks.

"Hey! What are you doing?!" I tried to stop him.

"Are you mad? So long we've been planning this lunch and of all days today you decide to do this?"

"Praveen!" I tried to reach out to the book as he placed it back on the rack.

"Everyone is so furious and poor Kriti is backing you like anything."

"Praveen stop!" I growled through clenched teeth.

But he wasn't stopping. He wasn't listening at all.

"You can do this easily on Monday."

Ignoring him I stretched out my hand to pull back my books but he blocked me.

"Praveen, listen. I have to do this today and I'm not going home before I finish it."

"C'mon, Oberoi! Is this more important than friends?" he whispered throwing up his hands in despair.

My heart winced a little.

However, my mind was set. I was determined to make my plan work.

"Come, let's go now." He moved a step towards me urging me to move towards the gate.

"No, Praveen. You go if you want to. I'm not stopping anyone," I said firmly.

"You can't do this, Oberoi."

"Watch me!" I blurted out.

Pulling out a few books from the rack behind him, I stomped across the library leaving him standing helplessly. A few seconds later, I saw him walk out of the library.

I sat down and opened the books to mark a few pages for photocopying. I had to wait till I was sure that my friends had left college and it made sense to utilize the time.

Twenty minutes later, having handed over the marked books to the photocopier section I headed to the canteen to make sure my friends had left.

Entering cautiously I scanned it and immediately heaved a sigh a relief. It was empty.

I decided to get a coffee before leaving.

Reaching the counter I called out for my order.

"Bhaiya, one hot coffee, please!" I shouted into the kitchen as he was nowhere to be seen at the counter. He came out hurriedly followed by someone and I was taken aback!

"Praveen?!"

He saw me and turned away.

"Yes Bhaiya, give her coffee. Busy people with so much work, you know. Give her lots of coffee."

Bhaiya laughed heartedly.

"I'll take two, please," I said to Bhaiya, smiling back.

Grabbing the cups, I thanked him before heading to my sulking friend. He had flopped himself onto a chair in one corner of the canteen and was pretending to read the newspapers on the table. I pulled up a chair and sat down across the table, pushing a cup towards him.

"What were you doing in the canteen kitchen?" I tried to start a talk.

"Having a lunch party with Bhaiya," he said sarcastically "and of course poisoning the milk that's right now in your coffee," he added as a matter of fact, pushing back the cup toward me.

"You didn't go with the others?" I enquired.

"No! I did. You didn't go with the others, Oberoi!" He continued to sulk. "And because most of us value friendship over books we decided to postpone the lunch."

I smiled, pushing the cup toward him again. He picked up the cup and took a sip. "And now I'm having poisoned coffee instead."

"Hmmm, I'm sorry Praveen," I mumbled. I really was but my plan had to happen today.

He looked up at me with a straight face. "Just sorry won't work. You've got to get me some maggi. I'm hungry!"

I laughed as he hid his face behind a newspaper. I knew he was smiling. Praveen couldn't sulk for long. I got up to place his order. My eyes momentarily darted towards the canteen door. On the road outside I could see a few students heading towards the canteen and amongst them, to my surprise was Raaghav!

I ducked behind the newspaper that Praveen was reading and pulled up the nearest chair.

"Hey!" he exclaimed. "What's wrong? You're becoming crazier by every minute!"

I covered my face with the newspaper.

"Whom are you hiding from?"

But there was no need for me to answer because at that very instant the group of students entered. Raaghav was easy to spot thanks to his amazing height and Praveen found him instantly.

"Oohhhh... So this is why you were not going for lunch today."

The reason behind my lunatic behaviour seemed to have dawned upon him. He let out a little laugh. "You could have just told us, Oberoi!"

"No! I just couldn't have told you..."

"Why?" He was perplexed.

Now what was I to answer? Why couldn't I just tell my friends that I was staying back for Raaghav?

"I don't know why!"

Raaghav had just ordered a bottle of coke. I could recognize his voice even in my sleep. For my surprise to be perfect, I had to remain hidden from him till the right time.

"Yeah, yeah... I know why. You're crazy for him. You don't need to have reasons to be crazy in love..."

"What's he doing?" I interrupted him.

"He's drinking a cold drink... but why are you hiding from him today? Generally you're all hyper and over active around him, trying to get in his way and doing all sort of antics for him to notice you. Don't want him to see you jumping today? Got a pimple or something?"

"Shut up! I have a plan for today."

"Wow! You ditch your best friends with a complete plan in mind."

I rolled my eyes at him! "I know you understand, Praveen."

"Of course I do! Friends got the right to joke, okay?" He laughed again. "But to be honest, I really admire your adoration for him. Completely head-over-heels and so blissfully happy! And you know what? You two look perfect together. Just don't let him get away ever!" he said in complete honesty.

I grinned at him.

"Are you going to take the newspaper home? Coz he's gone."

I put it down, just in time to see Raaghav entering the main building at the end of the road outside. I looked around. There were about half a dozen coke bottles on different tables.

"Which one is his?" I asked Praveen, a little thought creeping in my mind.

He laughed, pointing at the one on the table near the door. "Sure?"

"Dead sure! Are you going to take the bottle home?"

"Not at all! I was just asking. Listen, could you help me out a little?"

Now that Praveen knew why I had stayed back I decided to take a little help from him.

"Any time! Tell me."

"Without asking me why, could you drop me off at Shahdara metro station?"

He smiled and shook his head.

He said as he got up. "Let's go."

I smiled back, picking my bags while eyeing Raaghav's coke bottle.

"You go bring out the bike. I'll just clear my balance and catch up in two minutes."

"Sure!" he walked out whistling.

Quickly I cleared up my balance with Bhaiya and headed towards the coke bottle that had been calling out to me.

About a quarter of it was still full. I picked it up and slowly touched the bottle's mouth to my lips. Raaghav's lips had just touched this very bottle a few minutes ago and the thought was wildly arousing.

I kissed the mouth of the bottle before placing it back.

I had just indirectly kissed Raaghav.

I peeped at the entrance to the station again. His face was yet not to be seen. For the last few hours I had done almost everything I could do waiting at a metro station.

I checked my phone. The last message I had received from him was at 2 p.m. Must have sent it before beginning his lab work.

Hey! What's up?

To which I had replied that I had reached home.

Going to catch some sleep as someone who really likes me keeps me awake through the night, hinting at the sweet talks that I had so enjoyed last night.

Will call you when I wake up.

He had replied instantly.

Sleep well. 'Someone' misses you.

I smiled again as I read the message for the hundredth time since my arrival at the metro station. This *'someone'* was changing my entire life.

I looked at the message again.

'Someone' misses you.

I had deliberately not replied to it as the chat end had given me the perfect opening to this metro station surprise. But now I was starting to get a wee bit anxious.

He should have been here by now. What was taking him so long? Was he even going to go home by metro today? Or maybe he had planned some other conveyance! Suddenly I realized I had to find out where he was and I was struck by an idea!

I'd call him up. No, I couldn't call. The metro announcements would reveal my location. I'd message him! It had been a long time to cover my sleep and I could message him now. I typed in a message as quickly as I could and hit send. I looked up at the gate one more time and just as I blinked, came the moment I had been waiting for since morning.

Raaghav was here.

Tall, slim and sexy, he walked casually in his usual gait. Of course! He was a head turner any day! His bag was slung across one shoulder and his apron was hanging over his arm. His hair was super ruffled which he started to untangle as he stood in the security check line. I had a sudden urge to be the one untangling his hair.

I was overjoyed! He was here and he was alone! As he waited for his bags to pass the scanners, he took out his phone from the pocket of his blue denims. What a surprise this was going to... Shit! My thought was ruined in mid track as my phone vibrated. I realized I had just sent him a message and he must have replied to it.

I checked my phone – there was a notification message.

Message not sent due to insufficient balance. Please recharge.

Phew! Now there was no chance of him knowing I was here. I turned up and just managed to see him swipe his card for entry and head towards the lift.

I dashed to the lift doors on my floor and posed as casually as I could some ten steps away from the opening. I quickly put on my ear phones and crossing my arms on top of each other, I started moving my head slightly to the music.

Out of the corner of my eye I could see the lift doors opening. My heart was beating really fast. Someone stepped out and stopped. It was Him. I knew it was him.

I pretended to be lost in the song and did not immediately turn to face Him. He walked slowly towards me and just when he was about a feet away I casually turned towards him.

"Hey!" I exclaimed softly, taking out my earphones.

He was smiling and shaking his head. He looked stunned. And stunning too – all flushed up by the heat, his cheeks were the slightest shade of pink and little droplets of sweat were building up on the side of his temple. His eyes looked brighter than usual, maybe because they were open so wide and I couldn't help but resist darting my eyes across his slightly parted lips.

"What are you doing here?" He looked completely dazed. I was thrilled.

"Well, *someone* was missing me..." I stated referring to his message. "And I was missing *someone*... So here I am!"

He was staring at me as if he couldn't believe his eyes. All the wait, all the effort, all the time, everything seemed so damn worth it. Nothing could have been better than the reaction I was getting to experience right now.

"Other people are going to think you are a mad man. You're staring into air in the middle of the platform coz I'm actually not here... You're dreaming about me, Raaghav," I crooned dramatically.

He laughed out loud! He put out his hand and poked my arm gently with a finger.

"Okay, let's not get violent! You can hug me if you want to really check whether I'm real or imaginary," I suggested raising an eyebrow.

He was still reeling under the effect of the surprise.

"You came back from home?"

"Nah!"

A confused look spread across his angelic face.

"I didn't go back home," I explained with a shrug.

"Then where'd you go?"

"Nowhere. I waited right here. Right there actually." I pointed to my spot at the far end of the platform.

He followed my finger into space. Looked back at me and then turned to my space again. He stretched his neck upwards behind us looking out to something. I turned too – the platform clock. It was showing the time as 4:30.

He looked down at me.

"It's a Saturday today."

"Yeah," I smiled.

"You must have gotten free at 12:30. And you came here at?"

"Umm... Around 1:30ish..."

"Ira..." He paused, as if I had said something impossible, "you have been waiting here for the last three hours... for me?!"

"Well, yeah... I guess so..." I answered proudly.

"Ira, this is crazy!" The look on his face was reward enough for me. He was at a loss of words and I knew my gesture had touched him deeply.

He was smiling softly and then his smile spread all across his beautiful face. "I never thought people do this in reality... waiting and all. A girl waiting for a guy... Actually, a girl like you waiting for a guy like me!"

He was actually blushing!

"I don't know about what people do or not. But this is what I do. And someone told me yesterday that I'm very different from other people."

"You surely are! And I'm one lucky guy!" He flashed his million dollar smile that was bound to take my life one day.

"I'm luckier," I replied instantly.

We stood there staring at each other until the moment was broken by the hoot from an incoming metro.

"Shall we?" He gestured towards the metro with his free hand, ever polite and soft.

Picking up my bag and apron, I imagined spending the rest of my life with this gem of a person I had fallen so madly in love with. It was as if he had asked me the question of a lifetime... *Shall we be together forever?*

I smiled, answering softly.

"Yes, we shall."

Raaghav had spent the first ten minutes of our ride back home recovering from the stunning joy that my surprise had given him. He was of the belief that girls generally expect such gestures from the opposite sex rather than going ahead and doing it for them.

"But you surprise me endlessly... You're just so different, I never know what to expect from you next," he had admitted.

"I'll take that as a compliment."

"It is."

We had managed to get the couple seat in the metro – the one that is in between the door and the gang way. Raaghav had seated himself like a gentleman with no chance of any of his body part touching mine.

"So, how did you come to the station? And what did you do all this time? Tell me everything." His eagerness was adorable and once I began telling him about the day, there was no stopping me.

During all our talks on the phone I had found him to be a very good listener, but today talking at such length with him in person, my thoughts had changed. He wasn't a very good listener, he was a fantastic one!

He listened with his entire body. His head slightly tilted, looking into my eyes, following but not getting distracted by my hand gestures. Nodding as he caught up with my flow of thought and interrupting me appropriately with sensible questions that were coming in his mind. Smiling at the right time, laughing with me and most importantly, he did not rush me at all.

Forgetting to keep track of stations, we missed his. Or so I thought.

"We haven't missed it. I wanted to drop you off first and then I'll get back to mine. I thought it'll give us some more time together," he said sheepishly.

And all I could manage to do was smile back at him. He had the courtesy to drop me off even though I had imposed this ride upon him.

"What if I start coming back daily in the metro?" I asked tentatively.

"Then I'll drop you off home daily, of course! There are no two ways to that!"

"You'd do that?"

"Try me," he answered, running his hands through his hair throwing them back, but failing to do so. His silky hair loved to be on his fore head.

He was so enigmatic, it was baffling at times. One moment he's in college all straight faced and formal, but the minute he's out of college he becomes a different person all together – chirpy, hilarious and playfully flirtatious. But it was this very enigma that had me hooked on to him so madly. It was moments like these that I used to fall back on my bed while talking to him on the phone. I would close my eyes and imagine us together. But what was I supposed to do here in the metro? With him staring so deeply into my eyes.

Gosh! No matter how confident and smart mouthed I was, he had a strongly numbing effect on me. But before I could say anything, the station announcement caught my attention.

"That's me," I said sadly.

"Oh!"

We hurriedly got off the metro, managing not to get hit by the closing doors and as we walked towards the stairs, I sneaked at his face. He looked forlorn. I wasn't feeling too joyful either. I wanted to stay. I wanted more of him. I wanted more of us. Yet here we were walking down the stairs.

He was quiet. So was I.

Suddenly, he stopped mid track. I stopped too, a little startled.

"You must be hungry," he stated, instead of asking.

"Well... yeah, I am kind of hungry," I said, not understanding where this was going.

"Do you want to eat with me? Maybe a burger or something?" He pulled his ear while asking, as if fearing a rejection.

"You know what, I'm starving! Please take me!"

"So where can we go nearby. This is your neighbourhood, you tell me." He was rubbing his hands like an excited kid.

"No ways! We cannot go anywhere near here for the very same reason! It's my neighbourhood," I exclaimed, amused by his suggestion.

"Okay, so we're a secret that means." He was being quite playful today.

"You, of all people, have no right to joke about that!" I jeered at him.

He put up his hands in the air, "I accept it! I can't be the one joking on that point."

I laughed at his antics. All of this was so unexpected from him.

"All right! There is McDonald's at Kashmere Gate, if you're comfortable." His face all enthusiastic and vibrant again.

"Perfect!" I quipped happily.

"Okay listen, we need to cross over to the other platform and it's best if the guards don't see us," he said as we continued our descent to the bottom of the stairs.

"Okay!" I agreed, clueless about the reason behind his concern. I was going to McDonald's with Raaghav. The point where my brain would function normally to comprehend things as they were happening was long past gone. And my heart was of no use in such situations.

As we reached the ground, he grabbed my hand and pulled me across the corridor. I couldn't believe this was happening. Him holding my hand and pulling me to take me out to McDonald's with him! We literally ran across to the lift on the other side and he just managed to stop the doors from closing. We rushed in and heaved back against the mirror, laughing hard at our little devious run. As he continued to laugh into his free hand, my eyes darted to his other hand that was grasping mine. It was warm and soft.

My laughing stopped and I could hear my heart beating louder. I looked up to find him gazing at me – his green eyes reflecting darkly in the dull lighting of the lift. There was something between us. An electric tension that was wildly arousing.

And then suddenly the doors of the lift opened. We had reached the platform. As a reflex, both of us let go of each other's hands, smiled and walked towards the bench to wait for the next metro.

"That was something," I cooed softly.

He smiled staring at the ground between his shoes. The electricity that had built up in the lift remained but got a little diluted by the people and noise around us. And we began talking again.

About how I had lied at home that I might get late due to extra classes today, how he never had to answer to anyone at home no matter what time he reached, how boring it was for him to travel alone in the metro daily and so on.

It was no surprise how quickly time was passing and before we knew it we were at our chosen station, which again was one of the most crowded in the city. It was also infamous for being the worst station to de-board at for a girl in Delhi, thanks to the loitering gropers who would take advantage of the crowd to fulfil their sick needs. As I prepared to battle the incoming rush, Raaghav gently put his arm around my shoulder. I looked up at him and it was as if he could read my thoughts.

"You'll be all right, don't worry," he assured me. And for some reason I trusted him completely. I had blind faith in this guy. As the doors opened to the frenzied crowd rushing in, Raaghav had me covered. He firmly pulled me close to himself with the arm around me and I was amused as to how snugly I fit inside his partial embrace. With half his body behind me, and his free hand stretched out before us, he had managed to create a barrier all around and I was safely out of reach from any hands that could be ferreting around.

I had never felt that secure in such close proximity to a guy as I had felt today in his arms, or rather a single arm.

I was once again at a loss of words to express how I was feeling, and all I could manage to do was to thank him.

He smiled softly, "It is my responsibility to take care of you when you're with me. And doing so is my pleasure."

I smiled back, all flushed with joy.

"So, what are we having? I'm going to be dead in another thirty seconds if I don't put something inside here," he said patting his tummy.

"I'll have a McAloo Tikki," I replied, laughing out.

"Ditto! You save our seats here. I'll get the stuff," he called out before rushing off to the ever increasing line for order placement. I couldn't take my eyes off him. Well, I could, but I didn't want to.

Suddenly there was an urge within me, a burning desire that had been developing stronger since the past few days. I wanted to do something insanely ahead of limits. And I wanted to do it now.

He returned swiftly with two trays and settled them before me. My mind was still lost in its sudden pangs of wanting to do something crazy.

He was opening his burger and I put out my hand to pick up mine, while in reality I was ogling at his face so close to me. The one face I would imagine day and night around me. The only face which I wanted to kiss and caress and hold close to my heart.

And before I could think it over, before I could make sense of my action that was about to happen, before I could ascertain whether he'd like it or not, I went forward and did it.

Leaning in towards him I planted a big, wet kiss on his cheek.

"Hey!" he exclaimed loudly glancing around to see whether anyone had seen us or not.

He was in complete shock and awe, all together at once. He was blushing like a tomato, and I was pretty sure my cheeks were as red as cherries too. I started giggling as a wave of satisfaction crept gradually over me.

I felt gratified. He sat there gaping at me with his mouth open and hands in mid air, burger and all.

"Now, let's eat," I winked at him as I picked up a ketchup sachet.

Shaking his head, he quietly whispered under his breath, "Unbelievable, you are Ira," and smiled secretly behind his burger.

I knew he had loved it. It was written all over his face. And I felt strangely empowered and possessive at once. It was empowering to know that I had the ability to make him blush and go weak in the knees, but at the same time there was a sudden possessiveness that was blooming inside me. I wanted this power to make him blush only be mine. I wanted to be the only one to kiss him, and the only one who he would kiss back. Whenever that would happen that is.

My wild imagination gave no warning before leaping at the thought of us kissing each other. Apparently he was very conservative, and I had done enough for the day. I decided to focus on the food for once. My stomach was growling and this time it was an appeal for hunger. I turned all attention towards the tray and for the first time realized he had brought me a happy meal!

"Wow! How sweet!" I chirped with joy.

"I thought you'd never notice," he joked.

I rummaged through the box till I caught hold of the toy and gleefully pulled it out. It was a Hello Kitty the size of my ring finger, wearing a pink dress.

"Aw, it's lovely! Thanks!" I blushed as soon as I realized I was acting like a little girl. Avoiding eye contact, I picked up my burger and delved into it hungrily, glancing at him as I did so.

"Whoa! You're hungry!" He smiled while looking at the edge of my lips. It was only when he picked up a tissue and offered it to me that I realized I had gotten something on my face. Instead of taking the tissue from him, I put forward my face, obviously wanting him to do it for me.

He laughed softly and obliged.

There was something about Raaghav that made me want to open up to him completely.

Dropping me outside my society, he had called out to me just as I had turned to walk away.

"Ira?"

I turned back, looking up into his green eyes. It had become dark and the street lamp from above was just enough to illuminate his face softly. He was looking keenly at me with that soft sweet smile on his lips – perfectly pink, soft and endearing.

"Would you like to have lunch with me tomorrow?"

⌘

As I was walking across the metro parking, my phone buzzed.

I had a new message. Trying not to hit the cars, I paused at one corner of the parking lot and tried to read it, squinting my eyes against the bright sun rays reflecting off the screen.

You look beautiful. Let them fly in the wind.

It was from Raaghav. I jerked up my head trying to search for him. He had obviously gotten a chance to glance at me while I had been fighting with my hair. I let go off them and just as I started walking again, and caught him standing at the staircase. One look at him and I was oblivious to the world around me.

He had worn a black t-shirt with dark blue jeans and was leaning against the wall, one foot crossed across the other. One hand tucked into the pocket of his jeans, while the other hanging loose by his side. The wind had ruffled his hair too which he didn't seem to mind. As I walked up to him, I was taken aback by his action of reaching out to me and placing an arm around my shoulder. It wasn't for Raaghav to be so upfront.

"Hi! Just give me a minute here and I'll let go," he said casually, eyeing two guys on a bike. I nodded as we started walking, only to be startled by a crash behind us.

"So, I really don't need to mention how beautiful you are looking. Guys falling off their bike are proof enough," said Raaghav, pulling me slightly towards the stairs.

I giggled in his half embrace.

"And I don't need to really mention how possessive you are. Holding me close when guys stare at me is proof enough," I quipped.

We had barely reached the top of the stairs and he instantly let go of me, smilingly softly in his own little sphere.

"So, where are we going?' I asked merrily, excited about my very first official date.

"Well... We're not going to a place, rather places," he said stressing the plural reference. "You'll see."

I was delighted. In actuality it didn't even matter where we were going. As long as I was with him, I was as happy as I could ever be.

We boarded the metro, laughing at our antics of the previous day and settled into the couple seat. I was starting to feel that this seat could very soon become a usual place for the two of us. The idea of leaving my van and using the metro to commute to and from college crossed my mind. I decided to consider it and discuss it with Mom on top priority.

We reached the secret station very soon – it was the station where he used to de-board for his place. As we got of the metro, I caught his eye. There was a spark that little children have when you take them to the park. He sure was excited. And as of me, I was thrilled. I was on a date with Raaghav.

"So, what would you want to have for lunch?" he asked as we walked out of the station.

A street vendor selling corn on the cob caught my eye and I jumped eagerly. I just didn't know how to behave like a lady and with Raaghav around I was all the more casual. He seemed to like it as I could see from the expressions on his face.

"Let's begin with that?" I eagerly pointed to the corn vendor.

"Great!" The joy on his face was adorable.

As we relished the deliciously buttered corns, I suggested we indulge in only street food. He was delighted by it, adding on to say that he'd love to try out some joints he had been wishing to go to but couldn't find someone to go along with.

"Well here I am. This is me. There's nowhere else on earth I'd rather be!" I had joked and so began our touring around the streets. We spent a good two and half hours, pit stopping whenever a delicacy caught our attention. I never knew I had so much capacity to eat. And laugh either! Raaghav was hilarious!

All the eating was interspersed with a good amount of sightseeing too, and he enthusiastically showed me all the places he used to visit as a kid. He showed me his house too, from afar though, before heading over to a nearby park.

Dusk was falling.

"Do you trust me, Ira?" he asked suddenly as I sat gazing at the flowers, seeping in the bliss of the moment.

"Of course, I do!" I smiled back at him.

He got up and put forward his hand.

"Come."

I gladly took his hand – warm, soft and so snug around mine. We walked to the far end of the park where the lawns were gradually being replaced by trees. As the foliage got denser, I realized this part of the park was not as well lit up. It also seemed to be deserted. We continued to walk deeper into the thickening trees and the passage became narrower, until suddenly it ended. Raaghav turned around and looked deeply into my eyes.

"I have your trust, right?"

I nodded. He turned and we continued to walk, now off the pavement and into the trees. With my free hand I pinched my thigh to ensure this wasn't a dream.

No, I wasn't dreaming. This was happening for real. We reached a little clearing and stopped right in the centre. The night had set in and it was difficult to see the expression on his face. He stepped closer and letting go of my hand, turned me away holding me from the shoulders. I stared into the night seeping around me before everything went dark. He had covered my eyes with his hands.

I stood still.

"You need to wait for a few seconds," he whispered softly in my ear. In the coolness of the evening I could feel the warmth of his breath on the nape of neck and my stomach was knotting up.

"One... two... and three." He softly let go of his hands and what I saw took my breath away!

In the dark shadows of the trees, twinkling like stars were hundreds and hundreds of beautiful fireflies! Their light green hue glowing and fading across the stretch before me, finely orchestrated in a pulsating rhythm. I turned and looked around. We were surrounded by them as far as the eye could see. Softly shimmering fireflies dancing to the tune of some magical music that my human ears could not listen.

And I just stood there spell bound, so mesmerized by the extraordinary panorama that I almost forgot I wasn't alone. Looking back I found him standing a few steps away gazing in my direction. As I walked over to him, the winds around us grew stronger and the lighting show became more illustrious. Nature is responsive to human feelings they say. And everything around us seemed to be syncing to ours. The little clearing was softly flooding with moon light, while the winds around us were whispering sweet nothings. The trees stood around us as if waiting for something while the fireflies were already celebrating the moment.

We stood there gazing into each other's eyes, neither of us uttering a word. Both of us knew what we wanted yet the moment was not letting us progress. As if the universe had just one more thing left to complete the almost surreal moment in my life.

I took another step and he softly caught hold of my hands. Pulling me closer he placed one hand behind my back and my free hand landed right onto his chest. I was barely inches away from him and he stood towering upon me, looking deeply into my eyes. My neck stretched back I was leaning up to look into his face, the perfect angle I had always imagined.

And then it happened. Leaning down he pulled me closer into his embrace and planted a soft kiss on my lips. Lingering for just a second he removed his lips from mine, but paused close to my face, our noses touching.

Softly, he whispered, "I love you, Ira."

My eyes closed, I could hear the very feeling of love in his voice. This wasn't just any expression of love – this was different. This was Raaghav.

I opened my eyes and cupping his face, looked deep into his green eyes.

"And I love you, Raaghav."

Stretching up to him, my lips found his and we kissed again. Only this time there seemed to be no end. As I parted my lips, his tongue found mine and a thrill of ecstasy ran through my spine. I could feel myself merging into him as he embraced me tighter, my feet barely touching the ground. My arms were enwrapped around his neck, my fingers entwined in his silky hair.

And as if nature had left this for the very last, it gently started drizzling. As the cool water droplets hit me, the warmth of his embrace was all the more inviting. The passion doubled up and the clouds blessed us in the pretty night surrounded by twinkling fireflies.

Two lovers entwined in each other's arms, we kissed till it rained.

He stroked the back of my hand gently with his thumb, as I shuddered. Still unable to believe it, my mind once again replayed the moments I had just lived.

All the way to the metro station, the butterflies in my stomach had kept up their most energetic dance.

My very first kiss – warm, wet and passionate, had been out of a dream. And it had left me wanting more. No doubt, he wanted more too, as was apparent from his passion in the two lifts that we had taken up to the metro platform. Leaning back against the hand rail in the lift, I had him up against me. Feeling his warmth all over me, I had relished in our wet lock twice.

To say he was an amazing kisser would be an understatement. He was magical. He pulled me closer, rubbing my hand with his free one.

"You're cold," he whispered into my hair.

I was sitting in his embrace, my head resting on his shoulder. Completely drenched by all the rain, the cooling in the metro did seem beyond comfortable, but to be in his warm arms was better than any blanket. We were heading home. Not wishing to, but without an option.

I was too mesmerized to talk. The calm on his face gave nothing away but the way he was holding me spoke volumes. This was so new for me. I had always known him to be a reserved, shy guy and here I was, out on a dream date. I shuddered again and he hugged me tighter.

His cologne was intoxicating me like hell. And the warmth of his skin under his wet shirt was wickedly enticing.

Pulling myself together, I rose up as my station approached and we de-boarded the metro. Silently, knowing what both of us wanted, hand in hand, we walked and waited for the lift. I was enwrapped snugly in his half embrace – a perfect fit across my shoulders.

I felt so complete yet so incomplete. I wanted him more. I wanted all of him.

As we stepped into the lift, waiting for the doors to close, my breathing became shallow. My lips parted, in anticipation of the delicious kiss that I was about to devour, when suddenly a guy came running out of nowhere, shouting at us to hold the lift. My heart sank as Raaghav, the perfect gentleman, quickly put his foot between the closing doors.

Sighing I closed my eyes, letting my head hang down, as his grasp on my hand tightened. He felt my dismay all too well, and as if trying to make up, he planted a soft wet kiss on the back of my hand.

The pristine silence kept us mellow for the journey to my society, reaching where I quickly jumped off the rickshaw and walked away, without turning back. It was late evening and I couldn't risk being seen with a boy by the gang of ladies doing their rounds.

I entered the society gate, retrieving my phone from my bag – I knew he would call.

"Hey," I cooed into the phone.

"Hey," I could say he was smiling. "Long time no see"

I laughed!

"Yeah... Long time," I quipped, walking towards my flat.

"Don't go so soon, na."

I turned cautiously. He was nowhere to be seen. He must have meant otherwise, I realized. I turned back towards my block.

"Too late... I have to be home before the deadline."

"Yes, that's okay. You are home before the deadline. But, you can come down for a walk, right? I can still see you that way."

I stopped mid track in the stairs.

"You've not gone back?!" I exclaimed, whispering into the phone. I was too close to my flat.

"No," he calmly replied.

"Hold a minute," I paused at my gate, taking a deep breath to normalize my heart beat. Letting out the breath, I tried to straighten my face which was beaming with delight. So difficult this was – trying to hide my emotions! I took another deep breath and entered my house.

"Hi!" I waived at Ravi, plonked on the living room couch, He eagerly waived back, throwing me a full face smile.

"Where's Mom?" I asked, pretending to search the fridge for some water.

"Evening walk."

I almost choked on the water I was gulping. Mom would surely recognize Raaghav and she wouldn't need a second to guess what he was doing outside if she were to spot him.

"Downstairs in the society, you mean?" I asked throwing the bottle back into the fridge.

"Where else?"

Shit! I dashed out of the house and sprinted up the stairs, two steps at a time.

Mom was downstairs and so was Raaghav.

I quickly dialled in his number as fast as I could, while climbing the stairs hurriedly, reaching the terrace in record breaking time. The phone had disconnected and was refusing to reconnect.

Aaaaargh!

Stupid network! I had to tell him to get away from the society, wherever he was. I quickly sprinted towards the terrace wall overlooking the road on the left, scanning for two figures – Raaghav and Mom.

Separately, I hoped!

Mom was not there, neither was Raaghav. I wasn't kind of expecting him to be inside, but still I had to be sure.

I walked across to the wall ahead of me. No sign of either here as well. Moving right, I saw a pair of ladies walking towards the society gate, but a tree was partially blocking my view. I tried to sneak and just as their faces came into view, my body froze. It was Mom.

I hit redial for the umpteenth time, biting my lip in apprehension.

Please God, let it connect. Please.

And it connected! Hardly half a ring and Raaghav was on the phone.

"Thank God, you called! I thought...."

I cut him off.

"Raaghav, where are you?" My voice laced with tension.

"I'm outside your society."

"You can't be! Where outside? Which road?" I asked praying for it to be any road but the one that was parallel to the one on which Mom was walking.

"Umm... The one on the right side of the society gate. Don't worry!"

Exactly on the forbidden road!

"You don't understand! Mom is walking downstairs just parallel to that same road and we can't have her catching you here!"

"But she won't catch me! I'm a little farther away from your society."

"Where farther?" I asked, not convinced enough.

"I'm actually walking past the society behind yours," he continued.

I heaved thankfully.

I sighed as I caught Mom turning to the road towards the left of the society gate.

"Ira?" His voice was full of concern.

"Stay where you are. I'm coming."

"You're coming?!" He sounded excited all of a sudden. "But, you just said your Mom is on the rounds. And if that's risky for me, then is it not for you? I mean for us. I mean for..."

I giggled.

"Raaghav, wait!" I laughed into the phone, all fear from the last ten minutes dissipating into the fresh breeze playing with my hair. I jumped over a connecting wall, sprinting across the adjoining terrace, all the way to the far end. Peering over, I looked towards the road running parallel to the society next to ours. There he was.

"Going back home?" I quipped.

He turned suddenly. And then turned back again, expecting to find me on the road.

"I don't see you! Where are you?!"

"Up here!" I cooed into the phone, as he turned his gaze towards the terrace.

"Ahhh...." He smiled sweetly. "So, instead of downstairs, you chose upstairs."

He was standing behind a tree, staring up at me. The road was dark, but the street lights were illuminating him up perfectly.

I sighed.

"You should go," I whispered softly into the phone.

"I know. But I don't want to. I don't want to leave you."

There was truth in his voice. There was a complete acceptance of wanting me for him.

"I have to go home, Raaghav. You should go." My voice was becoming heavier as the feeling of his lips on mine was tearing me from within.

"Ira."

Listening to my name in his voice was ecstasy for me. It always gave me a high. And I always wanted more of it.

I closed my eyes repeating his name, sure to hear mine back.

"Raaghav," I whispered into the phone.

"Ira." His voice filled my entire existence. "Ira, I love you."

I wanted to open my eyes and look at his gorgeous face. But I kept my eyes closed.

"I love you too, Raaghav."

"I love you, Ira. I love you, I love you, I love you, I love you...."

And with every repetition, I could feel myself flying higher into the sweet dark night.

"Raaghav, if I look at you again, I'm going to jump off the roof. Please go," I literally pleaded.

"I'll catch you. I'll be your Superman."

I laughed out loud. I opened my eyes. He hadn't moved a bit, staring intently in my direction. I glanced over the society road, looking out for Mom.

"Okay, okay! I'm going! Supermom can be back any moment and Superman is not safe with her around, right?" He straightened up.

"I love you, Raaghav. Bye," I said before disconnecting the phone.

Looking up to the stars that had fulfilled my wish – my little wish of having love in my life, of having Raaghav in my life, I felt blessed. I closed my eyes to send a kiss to the stars, but just a second too soon.

Crash!

I fell sideways onto the platform before the stairs, landing on my right hip, my foot having missed a thick pole in the dark.

Something inside of my foot had broken.

Reaching home after getting my foot plastered, it had been a challenge to find a minute alone. The clock ticked away and our usual phone time approached while I kept wondering how to call him up.

Getting a minute with the landline on the living room was mission impossible.

Using Dad's mobile was absolutely out of the question – my conscience was dead against it for a zillion reasons of its own.

Mom's mobile, I wondered. Suddenly, I had a plan! I looked up from the book that I had been pretending to read. Mom was sitting on the other side of the bed.

"Mom, I think I'm hungry now," I muttered. The pain killers were making me all gaseous and nauseated, and the last thing that I wanted to do was eat, but now I had no other choice.

"Good, I'll get something to eat." She got up.

"Something light, please," I added meekly. "And oh, could you please give me your mobile? I need to call up Kriti and tell her I'm not coming tomorrow, or the van will keep waiting for me."

"Oh yes, you had better do that!" She tossed her phone towards me before leaving the room.

I casually dialled in the only number that I knew by heart. The bell rang. Once, twice, thrice.

C'mon, pick up!

"Hello?" Came a very formal greeting.

Ah! Thank God!

"Hi, it's me!" I whispered, fearing the proximity of the kitchen to my room.

"Hey!" He recognized my voice in an instant. "New number?"

"No, it's Supermom's!"

"Oh, really?!" He laughed.

"Yeah, really really. I had to use hers because while coming down from the terrace, I broke my phone."

"Oh! That's bad. So you're going to keep this phone for the night?"

"No! I can't!"

"Oh that's worse!"

"And what do you mean for the night? My phone will take almost a week to repair," I paused, wondering how to tell him about my foot.

"No worries! I have a new one at home which I'll give you tomorrow and you'll gracefully keep it."

"Umm... Raaghav, I might not come to college tomorrow."

"Why?" He sounded confused.

"I, actually... Ummm... I tripped slightly and... I... I hurt my foot... A little..." I tried to choose the safest words. "And Dad thinks I should rest it for a day, so..."

"Ira?" He cut me short. "What have you broken other than your phone?" His voice was brimming with concern.

"I tripped over a pole and broke my foot – my ankle ligament to be exact." I sighed into the phone.

He sighed too on the other side.

"It's plastered, isn't it?"

"So, just make sure that Ma'am knows I'm not going to be coming for the next few days, otherwise she'll get all freaked out," I pretended I was talking to Kriti as Mum entered my room with two slices of bread.

"Thanks Mom!" I deliberately said into the phone, so that he would understand what I was doing.

"Next few days... This is the worst." He sighed even more deeply. My heart was aching badly.

"I'm getting some tea as well. Have it while it's hot," said Mom before leaving the room.

"I'm sorry. I can't talk much. I just want you to know that I'm fine. Really, I'm fine," I whispered into the phone.

"You have a plaster on with a ligament injury and you're saying you're fine." He sounded ached too.

"Yeah, it's a green plaster. It'll heal me up super quick – just like my Superman's green eyes." I smiled at my plaster. "Now I need a number quick, from the student database of yours."

"Anything for you, my love," he said gently. "Have you had your medicines?"

"Yes, Doctor. I have had all my medicines, more than I think I should. Now hurry up! I don't have time – Kriti Khanna, 1st year."

"Well, the file needs to open up before I can search. So you're pretending to call Kriti, when in reality you don't even have her number."

"I'll have it if you would just hurry up!"

"K-R-I-T-I-..." he spelled out as he searched. "Ira, listen. I'll be waiting. Please call me back. Call me whenever you can. You know I'll be waiting. And I'll be waiting all night long." He sighed again. "I love you, Ira. Here, note down her number."

Knowing I'd hang up, he had sneaked in his thoughts. I quickly noted down the number he gave me at the end of my book.

"Try not to worry. I'll call you soon. Love you," I whispered quickly and hung up. I hated myself for being so curt, but Mom could be back any moment and my plan was only halfway through.

I quickly deleted Raaghav's number from the last dialled list and typed in Kriti's.

"Hey Kriti! It's me, Ira."

"Hey Ira!" she started slowly.

"Listen, I fell and got hurt today so I won't be coming to college for a few days. This is my Mom's number, coz my phone is broken. I'll call you whenever possible. Don't call me. And I'm in a real rush right now. Will explain it to you later, okay?!"

"Yeah, sure! Take care." She was all baffled. But I knew she understood my craziness all too well.

"Yup, I will. Thanks, good night!"

I sighed as I flipped the phone across the bed, going back to being absorbed in my book.

The next three days were terrible – I was in extreme pain and no matter how much hatred I had for pain killers, I was forced to take multiple ones through the day. Dad had decided to have me on leave and no matter how much I cribbed and cringed at his decision, his mind was made up. The pain was not as difficult to endure as the agony of losing my phone.

I was pining to talk to Raaghav. And I was growing restless and irritable at the slightest of provocation. To top it all, our last and amusingly first date had gifted me some pretty intimate moments of kissing. Reliving them had my emotions turned on strongly and I kept tossing and turning through the night, while Mom believed it was the plaster that kept me awake.

Finally, on the fourth day, I convinced Dad that I was feeling perfectly normal and that I really had to go to college. Two main reasons I had practiced upon, hoping for at least one to work. One was on the premise that I had already been on leave for four days and I was missing important lectures. This was least important as Dad was a man of priorities and at this point of time his was clear – my health. The other was actually a fact that I played up a notch – my plastered foot needed blood circulation, and walking around the house was not giving me enough exertion.

It worked. The next morning I was off to college. Off to Raaghav. My happiness knew no bounds. And in reality, I could feel no pain, no discomfort any more in my foot.

I was so excited to be seeing him after four days, I could barely restrain myself. As the first lecture ended, I rushed as quickly as I could with my plastered foot and settled in the arch of the door. Soon enough, the professor from the other lecture hall walked out and a crowd of seniors followed suit.

My eyes were in search of just one face. And I found him easily – with his height, it was always easy. All the tiredness of the past week seemed to have dissipated in an instant, just by looking at his angel face. He was bent over some notes, explaining something earnestly to the guy walking next to him. I knew he'd look up. I just knew. It was only a matter of when.

Look at me Raaghav, look at me!

He started climbing the stairs, his back towards me. And just before I would have lost sight of his face, someone standing at the base of the stairs called out his name and he turned. Only, he turned and stopped mid way – staring across the crowd directly into my eyes.

I smiled.

He looked stunned – shocked – amazed. I couldn't be too sure. But he surely was transfixed! The guy shouting out to him had almost called out his name thrice, but he just stood there in the stairs like a statue – mouth slightly open, eyes wide, staring out at me. It took him a complete minute to come back to his senses, that too when his friend reached him and pulled him away from my sight.

Along with Kriti's help, I slowly made my way to the canteen. On our way, I made up a story as to how I tripped over some bricks in my society and filled it up with some factual details. Kriti was overly concerned about me stressing my foot with all the walking, no matter how much I told her that I was feeling completely fine. I had a tough time convincing her to go attend the lectures. I'd join her in the lab period which was to follow.

"You'll not move a foot till I'm here to get you. Promise me!" she sternly said, handing me a cup of coffee, before rushing back to the main building. She was a real sweetheart.

I settled back into the stool, opening my black diary. My first date had me bowled over with a plethora of emotions and they had me strongly bamboozled since Sunday. I had to pen them down and I hadn't gotten a chance at home. Raaghav would surely come searching for me, but till the time he came, I decided to free my thoughts onto paper.

Gladly, in the company of my dear diary, I spent the better half of the hour. And just as I put back my diary, I turned to find Raaghav standing at the door. I smiled at him.

He smiled back but didn't walk up to me rather he went up to the counter behind me. I looked around the canteen. It wasn't empty. I stared at my coffee cup – Raaghav's fears resonating in the back of my mind, the fears that wouldn't let him open up to me in college. And just as I realized, he wasn't going to come sit with me I heard his voice behind me.

"Hey!" Soft and smooth, as always.

I turned softly, controlling myself, trying to behave professional. I noticed that a few guys sitting at the far end of the room were watching us.

"Hi!" I smiled softly.

"Here's the stuff that we that we need to courier back. The committee has a better supplier. And please ask them to call me," he said as a matter of fact, while handling me a plastic bag.

"Yeah, sure," I nodded, playing along in his act.

He nodded back curtly and without another word, walked away. The guys were whispering something which I chose to ignore. I quickly stuffed the poly into my bag, glancing at my watch – Kriti should be here any moment. I wanted to see what Raaghav had given me with such secrecy, but away from prying eyes.

Ten minutes later, settled into the lab area, I excitedly unpacked the poly to retrieve what was inside – a mobile phone.

I switched it on and typed in a quick message to Raaghav.

Hi!

Almost instantaneously, the phone started buzzing. Raaghav was calling. I disconnected it, peering across the test tube racks on my table, ensuring the professors were not nearby.

I'm in Physio. Can't talk.

He should have known I wondered. And too soon for it to be possible, I received a message.

You can feel the need to go the washroom any time!

I giggled into a corner as my partner came back with the stuff. Excusing myself, I limped over to the professor's desk and took my permission, dialling as I reached the washroom.

"Hey!" he sighed into the phone.

"Hey," I cooed back.

"How's your foot?" he asked softly.

"Much better since I saw you. And now that I'm talking to you, I feel nothing's been wrong at all." I flirted in full spirit.

"Mm hmmm?"

"Ya... Although, I think a kiss is what I really need to feel best.... Maybe, two or three."

I smiled at my green plaster as a sweet silence settled between us.

"You're going back by van right?" he asked.

"I don't wish to, but...."

"Please don't plan any surprises today. I want you to heal soon, so that we can have more dates."

"Yes, doctor." My giggling was back. I loved him as he was so caring.

His soft laugh on the other side was enough to make me sigh deeply.

"I love you, Ira."

Wow, this was un-imaginable. He was suddenly so expressive with me, that it was becoming hard to believe it was the same guy who I had been flirting unabashedly with for the past few weeks. The same guy who had walked out of a room fearing I may propose to him before a crowd. Three words from him and I was on top of the world – always.

"Love you, Raaghav. And mmmmmuuuahh!" I kissed into the phone. "That's the thanks for the phone."

A moment's silence and a sigh later, he softly replied, "That nearly took my life away. I think you should go back to your lab! Before I'm forced to come and take that thanks in person."

"I think I'd better wait for that happen."

"Ira..." he softly sighed.

And that was it. A new phase in our journey had just taken over and we became inseparable.

Our togetherness, which was at first only limited to telecommunication, soon become in person as well. My plaster came off soon and with some amount of convincing Dad, the metro became my new mode of commute.

The benefits of which, I choose to remain hidden.

As hidden as the journey I was on.

Young lovers are oblivious to the world around them, they say. True it is – cent percent.

The rush that I had been feeling was incomparable to any feeling I had ever experienced. We were head over heels in love with each other.

Shifting to the metro was the best decision I could have ever made and every single day became a date. The contrast – at college and after – added volumes to the fun in my love life.

On one hand was the formal relationship between us – college president and executive. We kept it so covered that we didn't even seem to be friends. The hidden emotions would consequently be revealed to me in the evening – in our alone time. They would be also be revealed with double the intensity as was apparent in our desirous physical pursuits.

One look at his face up close, one touch of his warm hand across my cheek, one pulling hug into his strong arms, one delicious wet kiss – all within the first few minutes of meeting him at the platform, was enough to dissipate the world around me. He became my world, I became his.

We loved travelling and every day we would explore some place new place in the city. Delhi Darshan was soon complete. The metro rides were fun in itself; with all the rush we'd usually end up sticking to each other and without saying, getting close was never enough. I'd take full advantage of the crowded metro and cling onto his broad shoulders while he'd wrap me up in one arm. I'd hang on it – the strength of the muscle knotting me up from the inside, conjuring sexy images of him before my open eyes. He'd often catch me blushing, reading my thoughts and he'd shy away, smiling softly. It wouldn't be an exaggeration to say that between the two of us, he was the more restrained and mature one.

It made him all the more alluring – guys like him were surely not made any more.

With him, I always felt safe and secure. I felt respected, loved and cared for. He knew what I wanted without saying and he was always in tune to my thoughts. We could talk about anything and everything in the world and not get bored. He knew how to make me laugh till my ribs hurt, and he laughed genuinely at my jokes. He'd sense when I was in a sour mood and it would take him seconds to revive me.

He also knew the exact point of my 'let's go insane' button and he'd push it frequently, partnering me in some really crazy fun – dancing in the rain, walking aimlessly for miles and competing endlessly at the video game parlour to win the big prize. He won it for me though – a huge, fluffy, brown-and-white dog with a big face and floppy ears. It was adorable and I named it *BigFace*. It became my sleeping buddy

Both of us turned out to be foodies – so there was a lot of stuff that we experimented with across the streets, relishing on the junk that we loved to refer to as 'survival therapy'. We'd go to restaurants and cafes too where we'd challenge our capacity to eat with dishes we hadn't ever heard of. It eventually boiled down to sticking to street food as it tasted the best and was pocket friendly too, considering that we were both limited to our pocket money. Also, he cooked really well and he'd frequently bring me lip smacking, home cooked delicacies. He knew the best in terms of studies too – he'd give me the most accurate tips on what parts to study, which questions to revise, whom to approach for the right mentoring and which professor to avoid. He was the perfect senior!

And of course, the most amazing lover I could have dreamed for. Time always seemed to be the factor that would end our daily outings and invariably I would be rushing late into the house – I was always out on the pretext of some project work, or extra classes or lab work. We were inseparable.

There was something between the two of us – a magical web or something that magnified whatever emotion we projected. Needless to say, the varied aspects of our relationship turned out to be quite vibrantly coloured than average - we were all into extremes.

Extreme talking – the distinction between day and night had blurred away long ago and we were perpetually connected; either in person or on the phone.

Extreme fun – our common liking for outdoor activities and travelling, coupled with a carefree and adventurous attitude at both ends.

Extreme PDA – which wasn't much in my opinion, but probably so in perspective of the people around us. More often than not we would catch being stared at by some uncomfortable fellow passenger in the metro.

Extreme kissing – French kiss, Eskimo kiss, lizard kiss, single lip, earlobe, shoulder, nape. We did it all, always in private. And it was never enough. Mostly it was divided between the firefly park and the expansive metro network, more of the latter. Specifically, because of just one reason – the lifts. While travelling across the city in the variety of metro lines we connected at the mental level, but in the little metal and glass box we connected physically.

But Raaghav was too committed to one archaic value, which I adored him for but hated equally. No matter how much I teased him or played with him, he was firm on this one principle of his

– no sex before marriage. Not that any of us had overtly talked about getting married to each other. Until, one fine day the much forwarded message that was doing the rounds landed up on my phone. It was sent by none other than Dr Green Eyes – the name I had kept unchanged in my phone list.

It was a list of words and the task was to add a name from my contact list in front of each and then send it back to the sender. I scanned through the words and sat back pondering over the words. Some I filled up immediately, but some I had to think a little deeply over. Five minutes later, I checked my framed message once before hitting send.

Best friend – *Kriti*

Partner in crime – *Motu (That's how Ravi's name is saved in the phone)*

Respect – *Papa*

Hate – *I prefer the word 'Dislike' –Vrishin*

Hug – *Dr Green Eyes*

Kiss – *Dr Green Eyes*

Love – *Dr Green Eyes (Do you still need to ask?!)*

Miss – *Mary (Little Miss Mary... ;D)*

Marry – *(Blank)*

Tossing the phone to one side of the bed, I went back to reading *Love Story* – the timeless story of tragic love, by Erich Segal. I had hardly managed to read half a line when suddenly my phone rang.

"Hey!"

"I have a couple of questions which I'm going to ask in decreasing order of priority," he started matter-of-factly. This was Raaghav defined in one word – straightforward. I smiled as I put away my book, switched off the bed side lamp and nestled deep into my blanket.

"Shoot."

"What do you mean by blank for marry?" he said blank as if it was a curse and he was utterly disgusted in having to say it aloud.

"It means I don't want to marry anyone," I calmly replied.

"Not even me?"

For a minute I thought I had heard something wrong.

"What?"

"Will you not want to marry me, Ira?"

Was this happening for real?

"Raaghav?" I framed an entire question by just saying out his name.

"Ira?" He played back my tactic. "Well..." he slowly spoke. "I wasn't expecting such a long wait for your answer. Maybe, I just framed it wrong," he continued.

"Ira Oberoi, will you marry me?"

I sprung up. He was actually proposing to me. And what an effect it was having on me. A minute ago I wrote an answer based on my firm belief against the institution of marriage and in an instant all my views had evaporated. How come I had never considered the possibility of marriage between us?

While I was rash, he was prudent. While I was bold, he was reserved. While I was silly, he was sensible. Where I was stormy, he was serene. While I was a sexy beauty, he was a handsome beast. While I was impromptu, he was patient. While I was brains, he was logic. We complimented each other just like coffee and doughnuts – sweet and bitter, together only better.

We made a perfect couple!

Suddenly, all I wanted was to marry him. I hugged up my pillow squeezing it to death.

"Tell me, Ira?" his voice soft, his poise unperturbed as ever. I could feel warmth in his voice and I knew what he wanted to hear. I picked up BigFace, rubbing noses with it.

"Hmmm... I'll have to think about it." I didn't want to say anything more for now.

"From a blank to 'thinking about it' in less than two minutes means you'll say yes in the next two hours," he concluded with conviction.

I giggled. My answer was pretty evident, and he knew it all too well.

"So now that it's clear that we're getting married, who's Vrishin?" he asked softly.

"Just a guy who lives nearby," I answered flopping back.

"And why do you hate him?"

"I don't hate him, as I mentioned clearly. Just dislike. Next question, please." I kept my voice as straight as I could. Raaghav could almost always read through my voice. And this was one moment I was not wishing to spoil by talking about Vrishin. Maybe some other time, but definitely not the day I had been proposed to by the love of my life.

He didn't probe further. "Okay, seems like you don't want to talk about him." Shit man! He could read through my pretence also! "No problem, whenever you're comfortable."

"Yeah, after all we're going to be together forever, now that it's clear that we're getting married," I cooed into the earphones that I had plugged on to prepare myself for sleep time.

"I love you, Ira."

"And I love you, Raaghav," I cuddled up like a ball into my blanket, as he filled up the night with soft whispers of sweet nothings.

He was more than generous with his love yous and kisses. And he wanted that many in return as well. I was gradually starting to see the sweet little boy in this man I had fallen for months ago.

It was as if our story had been written out of a fairy tale – sweet, magical and pristine.

How was I to know, that the fairy would lose her wand just as the tale was going to go for a spin.

I silently tip-toed into my room. There was a certain charge in the air that did not feel right. I opened my books and stared into the pages of Guyton's *Physiology*, trying to remember the events of the day.

Had I done something wrong in the morning? Why wasn't Mom acting normal?

My intuition had me on the edge. And it was starting to get on my nerves. I was getting rather uncomfortable with Mom's uncanny behaviour.

Maybe I was just thinking too much. After all, I was the one who was hiding heaps of personal information from her.

Yeah, that made sense. It would eventually turn out to be insubstantial by the end of the day, I reassured myself. Keeping all stray thoughts aside, I decided to get into the subject at hand. Examinations were approaching and it was high time I began any preparation. I searched for my class register in my bag.

It wasn't there. That was strange! As I searched through my desk, pondering over the last time I had attended Physiology class, it struck me!

I had changed my bag the previous day and must have forgotten my register in the old one. I got up to retrieve it from the chair where I had left it in the morning.

The chair was empty. I twirled around the room, but couldn't see the bag anywhere.

Wait a minute!

On one corner of the shelf in my room, folded neatly and piled up with a few other bags was my black bag. And it was empty.

It was then that the situation hit me like lightening.

I grabbed my bag and frantically searched for it in the hope of finding it. Front pocket, back pocket, centre chain. It was not there – my personal diary was not there.

I sank down onto the corner of my bed as the room started twirling around me. That diary had every minute detail of my love life – written in explicitly honest content. For me, it was an attempt to relive the moments that I used to cherish with Raaghav. There was absolutely no inhibition in the words or expressions that I used in the diary, freely letting the feelings flow. All our dates, our talks, our confessions, our first kiss and beyond – every moment of my relation with him was starkly described.

And as the pages of *Dear Diary* a.k.a. *DD*, swept across my mind, I was baffled as to how that phraseology would be digested by a person not of my age, belonging to a different era altogether and most frighteningly being *my* mother!

This was the reason why she was acting so weird. I knew beyond conviction that *DD* had come across her hands and for sure she had gone through it.

Shit! Shit! Shit!

DD had uncomplicated details of our private pleasures – it was exhilarating for me to indulge in penning down our surreal craze for each other. But while *DD* had preserved in it moments from all aspects of our life, what was threatening my sanity right now, was the elucidation of sensual gratification hidden in its pages. To say that I had been bold in my illustrations would be an understatement.

Our first date at McDonalds... That wouldn't upset Mum too much – a fleck on the cheek is barely getting physical.

Our first touch... Hmmm... Now the point of touch was of concern....

Our first hug... Too many points of concern!

I shivered! And as the remaining pages flashed across my mind my feet started turning cold. Our very first kiss... Second, third, endless kisses, intimate descriptions of second and third base progressions – every minute detail had been dearly adorned in the pages of *DD*.

What an idiot, I was! Which sensible person writes such things in a diary!

And who ends up leaving such a diary unattended at home in reach of one's mother! A traditional, conservative, orthodox, died-in-the-wool mother!

I was a complete buffoon! I wanted to hit myself on the head with something hard – partially for the halfwit that I was and partially in some hope of getting up from this horrible nightmare!

Thank God for Raaghav's commitment on his archaic principle of no sex before marriage! An account of that in my style would have rendered *DD* as a revamped version of *Kamasutra*!

My mind was reeling. My heartbeat had accelerated to 280+ and I thought I was going to have a heart attack.

Holding my head in my hands, I tried to calm myself down. I needed to analyse the situation.

I needed to talk to Raaghav. I sprang up, pocketed my phone, put on a hair band and wrapped a stole around my neck. Pausing at the door, I took a deep breath and tried to fake an expression of indifference. I exhaled and turned the knob open.

I ventured into the living room and out of the corner of my eye I could see Mum working in the kitchen. I causally stated aloud, "I'm going for a walk."

Mum did not call out at all and neither did she stop me from leaving the house. She was surely restraining a storm within her and an outburst would be inevitable.

I was doomed.

I had to be out of sight from my flat's windows just in case Mum was sneaking up on me. With as much of a casual attitude that I could manage I walked across the road towards the lane leading to our society park and barely after turning the corner I hit speed dial. The bell rang just twice before it was disconnected and in an instant, my phone was ringing.

"Hello," I answered quietly putting the phone to my ear.

"Hey!" His voice soft and calm, as usual. "I got so engrossed in studying that I completely lost track of time... I'm sorry....!" he cooed.

"That's totally all right." I tried to compose myself. He had an exam tomorrow. Not a major one but an exam still. Should I tell him or... I did not really have an option though. Mum was surely going to bring up *DD* tonight and I needed him to know the situation in which my stupidity had put us into.

"Good you called. I was starting to lose my brains in all this Medicine."

"Sweetheart, is everything okay?" he asked softly. I knew it wouldn't take him a minute to know.

"Ummm... There's something I need to tell you," I murmured.

"Tell me baby... Are you all right?" His voice was laced with concern.

"Shit! I've gotten us into a problem, Raaghav! A big *big* big problem! And I just don't know what to do now! And this is all

134

my fault! I'm so stupid! And I.....” I blurted into the phone in one breath before he interrupted me.

“Hey! Hey! Calm down!” His calm had not been perturbed one bit. “Relax Ira... Tell me slowly and clearly.”

“I *am* an idiot!” I said throwing up my free hand in exasperation. “I have a diary and I write everything that comes to my heart in it. All the times that we meet and whatever we do, I like writing it down... In detail... And in true exact feelings....”

“Mm-hmm...” He patiently urged me to continue.

“And that diary has gone into Mum's hands!” I almost cried into the phone.

“Hmm... So, what did she say?” he asked still calm.

“She hasn't talked to me yet!”

“Okay...” He was trying to make sense of the situation. “So, how do you know she has the diary?”

“Because of *my* stupidity!” I whimpered into the phone and bent over my knees as I sat on a park bench.

A tear rolled down my cheek. Now I was losing it.

He gave me all the time I needed.

“I'm listening,” he gently spoke across the phone.

“Remember my black bag?” I asked him blankly.

“Yeah...”

“It had gotten really dirty and I had changed it yesterday,” Somehow, I brought myself to speak slowly and coherently. “What went wrong is that I completely forgot to empty it and now Mom has found the diary.”

“Hmmm... So the diary has *all* the details about us?”

“Yes.” It was all I could manage.

“Everything?!” The way he stressed on *every* suggested a hint of amusement in his voice.

“You're not scared?” I demanded bluntly.

“No, I'm not scared,” he said calmly. “I've loved you truly, and I like to believe that you love me too...”

"Of course, I do!" I interrupted him.

"So, what is there to fear? Ira, listen, I love you..."

I sighed into the phone. Somehow, I didn't want him to know my feelings. "I know. I'll handle her... I just wanted you to know all this because she's surely going to talk over it tonight... So, don't call me... Please..."

"Why not just let me be on the phone so that I can hear what goes on..." he suggested.

I wanted him to speak more and it was just not happening. And I just didn't feel like saying anything more. After about what seemed like infinity he spoke softly, "I'll wait for your call..."

"It might get too late... The talk might take long... I don't know..." I murmured into the phone.

"No matter how late, you know I'll be waiting, Ira," he replied softly.

What a mess. And just when things were going so smooth and lovely, I had to make this blunder of my life!

I didn't know what to say and deciding not to prolong the agony of this conversation any more, I hung up with a mere 'hmmm', without even waiting for his acknowledgement of the same.

DD was mine and I had been the blockhead to go ahead and fill it up with uncompromising details of our love life. I had put myself into this muddle and I was the one who had to deal with it.

After all, like he had just said there was nothing wrong that I had done. Whatever I had done had a logical backing. This was the guy I loved – completely, madly, deeply and forever. It made perfect sense to move ahead and get personal. So what, if I was only nineteen years old?!

Suddenly, there arose a feeling of anger and resentment within me. And I knew where it was stemming from... This was not *my* fault!

This was all Mom's fault!

How dare she open my bag and read my personal diary without my permission?! I mean, that's what a personal diary is supposed to be – a *personal* record of one self. Not for anyone and everyone to read when they came across it! How dare she consider it a right to open and go through *DD*!

With firm resolve I headed up the stairs to confront Mom.

As my hand reached out towards the door knob, I could hear her voice from the inside. She was talking to someone about something. Must be on the phone as it was only her voice I could hear. I wondered who it was coz she generally did not talk to anyone so late in the day... Who cared, anyway!

I was going to call her in and demand my diary back.

Determined I turned the knob and pulled the door. She was sitting on the couch and as I entered she went quiet and turned to face me. She wasn't on the phone.

I walked in and as the couch came into full view, I realized who she was talking to.

Dad was home.

Shutting the door to my room, I took the longest breath I had taken since ages. Crossing the living room had been nerve-racking.

Why was Dad home so early today? What was Mom telling him so gravely? Was it about what she had read in *DD*?

The anxiety was back with a vengeance.

Dad could not know about it. He was way too conservative and orthodox to accept such behaviour from his daughter. He would probably just get a myocardial infarction knowing about it! Mum knew that too... She had known Dad long enough... She wouldn't tell him for sure.

No! She definitely wouldn't tell him about it!

Pacing up and down the room, my hands had turned red from all the wringing.

I was getting tired from all the worrying and fretting and as I was about to slump into my chair there was a sudden knock on the door – I literally jumped out of my skin!

"Dinner," Blunt and monosyllabic, Mom was really setting up her scene well.

"Not hungry," I tried to sound as unaffected as possible.

There was a tornado in full swing under the skull of mine and it was disrupting all potentially required weapons that I needed to fight.

I needed food – but I was not feeling hungry.

I needed logic – but I had never felt crazier in life.

I needed words – but my mental dictionary had also disappeared.

Never before had I faced a situation vaguely similar to the one at hand. Mom hadn't been very approving of Raaghav since the beginning. That was probably the reason why I had reduced talking about him before her and *DD* had taken birth.

As I sat staring at the open pages of Guyton's, the sound of Ravi's cartoon show filled the room – someone was opening the door. In my peripheral vision I got to know it was Mum. She came in and closed the door behind her, shutting out the noises from outside and a creepy silence fell over my room.

I pretended to be unaware of her entering my room and scanned the lines on the pages.

"Yes?" Her voice was curt and cold.

I turned suddenly, pretending to be shocked.

"Whoa!" I exclaimed! Turning to look at her I added, "When did you come?!" and then deliberately turned back to my book, faking deep concentration.

She walked up and came to stand at the side of the bed. Folding her hands on top of one another – the perfect sign of closed body language, she asked, "Is there something you want to tell me?"

What?! That was too blunt.

I continued my act of reading and stated casually, "Na... Exams are nearing, got to study."

Out of the corner of my eye I saw her walk towards the storage cabinet in my room. She opened it and took out something. Her back was towards me but in her action of retrieving the thing from the cabinet I caught a glimpse of *DD*. My heart was beating like a huge drum against my rib cage and I feared it would burst.

As I tried to bury myself into the book, petrified of the event to follow, the name of the chapter suddenly caught my eyes – Chapter 22, Cardiac Failure.

Definition of Cardiac Failure – The term 'cardiac failure' means simply failure of the heart to pump enough blood to satisfy the needs of the body. Well in that case my heart was fit and fine! It was pumping way too much blood to satisfy my body needs – the warm flushing that I could feel in my cheeks was all blood for sure!

"What's this?" Finally, came the words I had been dreading all evening.

I deliberately delayed my response, pretending to finish a line and then looked up to her. She was standing just near the cabinet, holding *DD* before her. My game had to start now!

"Where did you get that?!" I exclaimed, feigning perfect shock! I turned around in my chair to face her and the look that met my eyes was one of utter disgust and contempt.

I didn't let her answer.

"You cleaned my bag?! And took out my diary?" I generously laced my expressions with accusatory revolt. "How could you?"

Her answer was instantaneous.

"How could *I*?! How dare you!" she mumbled through grated teeth. "I should be the one asking how *could* you?! Everything written in this... It's true or is it made up?"

Seriously?! This was her ray of hope? That her daughter imagines falling in love with a guy and pens down their lascivious feelings in a diary?! This was utter disrespect to my precious emotions captured in *DD*. All fear inside me had suddenly disappeared and the anger that was boiling me a few minutes ago was back with a storm – I was seething!

"That..." I paused and pointed at *DD*, looking at it to stress upon its importance for me. "Is *my* diary... And you had no right to read it." I tried to control myself from screaming into her face and so the words came out with extended pause and pressure. But my effort to talk normally was a waste.

"*I am your bloody mother*! I have all the right in the world to know *what you are doing*!" she bellowed. "And this is what you are doing? *This is what we send you to college for?!*"

"That's my personal life!" I screamed back, trying to fight back the tears that had welled up.

"*And no matter what you have no right to read anyone's personal diary! It's called a personal diary because it is supposed to be personal*!" I went on hissing. "These are my private feelings and I don't need to share them with you!"

"*You have to!*" she shouted back.

"*Why should !?*" The tears were flowing freely now.

"Because he's a *******! He's using you and will throw you away once he's got what he needs!"

"He loves me!"

"This is not love! This is lust! This is bullshit!"

She looked down shaking her head slowly. My mind was reeling under what I had just heard – this is what she thought of her daughter's love – Bullshit.

Suddenly, everything around me was becoming dark. My brain had shut down. I could no longer feel the intense throbbing of my heart. I sat there staring at the ground below – completely numb.

I tried to blink, but it dint happen. I tried harder. My eyes shut down and I was somewhere else. I was with him.

Walking down the lanes of the fireflies park, hand in hand...

I opened my eyes. Closed them back.

Holding on to each other in the metro...

I opened my eyes and closed them again.

Laughing over something... Hugging in the lifts... Dating at McDonalds... Kissing in the rain...

I don't know how long I was lost in my trance but I was being brought out of it now by Mom hugging me. She had not stopped speaking, but not one word had registered upon my deaf ears.

"I failed as a mother," she regretfully whispered in my ear. "I couldn't make my daughter strong enough. If you would have been stronger you would have never succumbed to his filthy demands. Don't worry. You no longer need to be scared of him. If he forces you, just tell me. I'll handle him."

The darkness around me was becoming thicker. I felt I was suffocating. I wanted to shout at her. I wanted to cry. I wanted to scream my lungs out. I wanted to run away. But nothing happened – I just sat transfixed.

She kissed my forehead, picked up *DD* from the bed and placed it in the cabinet, locking it.

The next moment she was gone.

With a blink I came back to my senses.

For how long I had been sitting frozen in my chair, I had no idea. I stood up, looking around my room, searching for something. I picked up the blankets throwing them aside. Pulled up the sheets and stuffed them into a corner. I searched below my pillows and behind the curtains. I couldn't find it. I slumped back into my chair.

What was I searching for?

My mind wasn't responding. This was not good.

Shuddering, I sank down onto the heap of blankets, as the reality seeped in. In an instant I knew what I had lost and what had hurt me – I had lost Mom's trust and the shame I had bought upon her is what was hurting me.

Burrowing my face into the darkness of the blankets, I screamed like a maniac, my heart ripped apart. Fallen on the ground – broken and defeated, I cried till no more tears came out.

The sound of the clock fell on my ears through the deafening silence around me. I looked up. It was past midnight. I had been alone for more than four hours.

I got up. My legs were quivering and I was feeling cold. The room was a mess around me. I started cleaning up. Meticulously, I arranged everything back in its place and tidied up. Once done, I quietly opened the door – it was dark outside.

Everyone had gone off to sleep. I walked up to my favourite couch in the corner of the living room and sat down on it.

My mind blank, my heart still and my eyes dry.

I just sat there lost that I did not realize when Mom came out from her room.

"I wish you wouldn't have done it," she stated through clenched teeth, as I jumped out of my skin.

She was pacing up and down the living room, mumbling incoherently or maybe I was just too numb to understand what she was saying. I tried to blink away my tears which had suddenly returned with a vengeance.

"I knew I'd have a heart attack in my life!" she shouted suddenly and I caught my breath.

I realized she must have been constantly thinking about the descriptions decorated in *DD*. She must be freaking out.

"Mumma, please relax!" I tried keeping my voice calm. On the inside I was breaking apart but I didn't want her to see it.

"What a horrible shame! What all had I expected from my daughter and this is what I have today! We spent lakhs in trying to make you a doctor, a respectable person. And this is what you do in college?! How could you?! I tried to make you a strong girl and you let yourself be used by a boy! You have failed me as a daughter! I feel sick when I am reminded of the things that you have done! Horrible! Horrible! I knew my health wasn't going to keep up. It was written since long in my destiny. But how was I to know my very own daughter was going to be reason behind it!

What a shame!"

She was completely out of control. Her hands exaggerating her words, her voice filled with disgust and hatred. I was starting to panic now. This kind of anger was not good for her.

Mum hadn't switched on the lights. She probably didn't want Dad to be awakened.

"I cannot even imagine doing these things with a stranger. And you have gone ahead and... God damn it! How could you?!"

Tears were flowing freely now onto my cheeks and into my hands. As my lips started quivering, I pursed them together and closed my eyes tight shut.

"Why? Why did you? Why? Oh God, I can't take this anymore!" her voice barely audible.

I looked up and saw her swaying a little. I rushed to her side and caught hold of her just in time, as she fell.

"I fear if Papa gets to know all this! He will surely kill you! Oh, God! Why did you have to do all this?"

"Mumma, please relax. It's all over now. Please," I pleaded, speaking up for the first time since she had come. The look on her face was terrifying. She wasn't fine.

My heart was pounding like a drum and I could hear the beats ringing in my ears.

"Please relax." I tried to calm her down.

But she wasn't listening to me.

"I did everything that I could for you and this is how you reward me! By failing me! By killing me!"

She took a deep strained breath and tightly grasped her chest over her heart. Her eyes winced in pain as she fell back, leaning against the couch.

"Mumma! Mumma! Mumma!"

I thought she had fainted. She looked up, breathing heavily.

"Just leave me alone. I don't want to see your face," she whispered, pushing me aside. I stumbled back a little, trying to assess her condition.

She stood up and took a couple of deep breaths. I took a step towards her but she raised a hand, clearly signalling me to stay away.

"Just call him tomorrow and end all this." Shaking her head, she slowly walked back to her room, leaving me standing in the middle of the room.

Cold, alone and heartbroken, I went back to my room.

Watching Mom falling to the ground, fearing she was having a heart attack was enough to restart my brains. I had made up my mind. Picking up my phone, I called him up.

"Hey!"

"I can't do this anymore, Raaghav. It's over." I was speaking like a robot – emotionless and bland. I was listening like one too, unable to discern the emotion in his voice.

"It can't be over."

"It is. I can't do this."

Silence, long enough for me, filled up the gaping distance between us.

"I'll wait for you, Ira."

The next second I disconnected the phone and switched it off, along with the lights of the room.

I shut tight my eyes. Vivid images of love laced moments. In the warmth and solitude of the blanket, my heart ached to be with him again – if only through memories, then so be it.

The bitter pain was the only thing that was making me feel alive at the moment. My entire love story streamed past my closed eyes, again and again and again, till it felt like falling into an endless abyss. And just when I thought I was about to burst with all the emotions raging inside me, it all evaporated into the darkness.

Blank and fatigued, I fell onto my bed, and went into what felt like a coma.

Present day

My sleep was broken by soft voices – songs of love and happiness. I could feel the warmth of the sun shining on my face and I tried to cover up my head with my blanket. As I pulled it up, it left my feet uncovered, which fell to the ground as the world around me jerked. I woke up in a daze!

The bus had come to a screeching halt. I looked around absorbing the details of the scene around me. Of course, I was in the bus en route to Ludhiana and we seemed to have stopped for breakfast. Brunch rather, it seemed as I glanced at my watch. Students had already started de-boarding up front. I turned towards the aisle – cautiously avoiding the back seats, just as Manvi turned to face me.

"Good morning!" she crooned still in the tune of some song that she had been singing, along with my other friends.

I smiled, wishing her back as I tied up my hair in a bun.

Out of the corner of my eye, I saw the last seat was empty. He must have de-boarded already – rather, he must have been the first to get off – head of responsibility, after all. I paused at the bus door, breathing in the freshness of the open fields, soaking in the warmth of the sunshine.

Such a contrast to that dreaded night. Putting away my thoughts, I entered the fantastic village styled restaurant, named appropriately as 'Haveli'.

I looked around. It was huge, dimly lit and well decorated, decked up with little lamps and traditional cots. My friends were already taking snaps – faces all puckered up and pouts well defined. I smiled, seating myself onto one of the cot, glancing at the menu.

"Can I get you something?"

I froze, hearing his voice right behind me. I dared not turn.

"Thanks Raaghav! Just a fresh lime soda for me," answered the accompanying faculty. She must have sat down just at the adjoining table. I rushed out of the restaurant, breathing heavily, every muscle in my body tense. The winds gushed across my face as I walked up to a small counter and ordered a glass of salty butter milk, just as Manvi came up from behind.

"Make that two, please," she chirped, holding me by the arm.

"Everything's fine, don't worry." She smiled at me, knowing the truth all too well. But I had her promise.

The students were mostly spread over the vast expanse of Haveli. I walked around aimlessly, trying to keep my mind distracted. In one corner were a few traditional activities – pot making and henna art, along with a tiny stall of bangles and embroidered artwork. Simar and a few others were bent over the stuff, haggling with the vendors. Just ahead of the stalls, there were some local ladies dancing to the dhol, surrounded by a few guys from our bus. Anjali's shrill voice cut through as she called out, astride a camel waving like a little kid.

I waved back, laughing with her, as she crossed across the dance group towards another stall which caught my eye – face painting and tattoos. I casually strolled towards it, only to be stopped in mid track. Someone was getting something painted, just not on his face, rather on his hand.

I stopped mid track, a painted hand from the past filling up my thoughts.

Turned around with a jerk I accidently bumped into a tall figure. I didn't need to look up to know who it was – the cologne was enough to have me intoxicated within a fraction of a second. Ducking to one side, I swiftly walked past, straight into the bus. Soon enough, it started moving and the voices around me started fading. Raaghav was slowly walking down, making sure everyone was on board. I looked away, resting my head against the window, at the green fields zipping away.

Particular and fastidious – just as he had always been even on that fateful Teacher's Day Celebration. Closing my eyes, I drowned back into my reverie – our last event together.

⌘

3 months ago

It had been over a week since I hadn't gone to college. With all the drama at home, coupled with a complete loss of time synchrony, it had become impossible for me to get back on track. My phone had been off since the night I had tossed it aside. Kriti had called up on the landline, worried after three days. I had told her I was down with the viral and my phone was not working.

To be back in college felt as if I was walking on broken glass. I must have seemed low and in an attempt to cheer me up, my friends would talk only about Raaghav. For them it was the best method to have me gushing with happiness and dancing around in joy. How were any of them to know the truth? While they still thought about my love interest as a crazy one sided attraction, the real story of my heart had gone full circle and was now at the brink of an end. With all their good intentions, they continued to jeer me and tease me about Raaghav and my heart bled like water.

I simply smiled through it all, claiming to be low on energy because of the fever. I was a good actor. No one doubted my excuses, ever – except for Raaghav.

Quitting the committee had already been considered. I just had to find Deepa Ma'am and inform her. But before I could utter a word she ran away in a rush, shouting out behind her, "Committee meeting, right now – LT 3."

I spread the message across, contemplating on ditching the meeting. I just wouldn't be able to stand it – having him so close, hearing his voice. Instead of walking into the LT, I walked past it and busied myself in the library for the next two hours – long enough for the meeting to be over.

Later, I entered the canteen to find out it was for Teacher's Day. I realized most of the preparations had already been completed. In one corner, a couple of tables had been pulled together and were filled up with all the decorations and gifts for the teacher awards. The creativity team from our class – four chirpy girls were all over it, along with a few other members of the committee. Of the four, I knew only Manvi slightly better – she was Raaghav's Rakhi sister, as he didn't have a real one. Suddenly turning towards me, she signalled me to come over. I was taken aback. I really didn't know well enough to deserve the smile she had just flashed over at me.

I walked towards the elaborate arrangements going on, mostly concerned with the one common gift being made for all the department heads – a hand crafted book shaped box with a Parker pen fixed in the middle of each. As I reached up, Manvi handed up me some sheets and scissors, beaming at me like a clown.

"Some help, please?"

I didn't want to but her smile was too charming to just refuse. Sighing, I dropped down into the vacant chair next to me, smiling softly at the other three girls – Simar, Anjali and

Devi. They all smiled back, warm and sweet, guiding me on what had to be done with the sheets.

How come I had never even talked to this group of my batch-mates? I didn't need an answer though. I already knew it – my obsession with Raaghav had kept me more than occupied to be aware of the people around me. A second later, my hand with the scissors froze in mid air as my obsession walked in.

Busy talking to the guy with him, showing him some papers, he walked straight towards us. I looked around, searching for a convenient route to escape. There was none. I looked back towards him and our eyes met. He was alone now. He continued to walk towards the tables, eyes fixed on me. I continued cutting the sheets.

"Ira, I need to see tomorrow's speech."

Whoa! I looked up as everyone around me remained engrossed in their work, but I managed to catch Manvi staring at us. She hastily turned away.

I looked back towards Raaghav.

"Library, ten minutes." Curt and direct, he walked away. Just as he reached the door he turned back, "Manvi, bring along a sample box also." Our eyes met again before he disappeared behind the wall.

There was no speech, we both knew it. I looked around the table. Everyone seemed to be busily engrossed – smartly done, Raaghav.

I once again caught Manvi staring at me, smiling softly. And it struck me like lightning. She knew about us – about me and Raaghav. Suddenly I felt infuriated. I hated double standards! While I was not allowed to share the depth of our relationship even with my bestie, he enjoyed the right to tell everything to a Rakhi sister.

Manvi was by my side in less than a second, "Coffee?"

The look on her face was a pleading one. As if she wanted to say something. Reluctantly, I walked with her towards the counter.

"Please don't be angry at him," she said as we sat down at a table.

What? Was she a psychic?

"Your face is so pure – your emotions are easy to read on it." She smiled innocently.

I stared down into my coffee.

"BigB... I mean Raaghav Bhai is like a brother to me. We don't talk much but last week he called up and..." Her voice faded away.

I looked up. It was her turn to stare into the cup in her little hands. She looked up, sighing deeply.

"He was so worried about your phone switched off and no news of you – I talked to Kriti and updated him. He didn't have to say a word. I knew what was going on just by the concern in his voice."

"You have no idea," I scoffed.

"Maybe I do. Ira, please meet him once. You at least owe him that."

My heart was sinking. I gulped down the coffee in one go, standing up. I strode out of the canteen, heading not towards the main building, but towards the college exit. I could hear Manvi shouting my name as she ran up behind me. Just before she could reach me, I turned abruptly.

"Dilshad Garden metro station. Tell him I won't wait till four."

I left her standing next to the solitary tree in the park, as I walked out of college.

The second metro skid by as I stood at our spot on the platform – resting against the pillar. Manvi had been right. He did deserve answers to whatever he wanted to ask. I knew he would come. It was only a matter of when. I looked at my watch and raising my head, I saw him climbing the stairs. He walked over to where I was standing and leaned back against the pillar. I looked straight into his green eyes – sad, lonely and hurt. I didn't blink, but gulped down the big lump forming in my throat.

"Why are you doing this Ira?" he managed to whisper.

I answered it with as much resolute that I could muster.

"Raaghav, Mom got to know things about us that she would have never dreamed from me. I have made mistakes. I've exploited the liberty given to me and crossed lines I should have never even approached. I'm lucky she's given me a chance to correct myself. And that's just what I'm doing."

He stood listening patiently, his face wearing an expression of extreme helplessness. We stood silent. He just kept staring at me, while I tried to avoid eye contact.

"You're looking beautiful," he said softly.

I rolled my eyes, wishing I could punch him in his ribs.

"Raaghav, please don't make this more difficult than it is already for me."

"Is it?" A ray of hope gleamed in the tear filled emeralds.

"Shouldn't it be?" I stared back into his gaze, every inch of me wanting to hug him.

He slowly took my hand in his, rubbing his thumb across the back of my palm. I involuntarily closed my eyes.

"I love you, Ira."

My lips were quivering now, but I had vowed not to cry – at least not before him. I silently took deep breaths, freeing my hand.

"Raaghav, I can't be yours till we get settled in life – that's what is normal and acceptable in our society. And so it is for Mom.

"I should be focussing on my studies, becoming a doctor. That is all they have ever asked of me and my distractions towards you is putting their dream at risk. I am only nineteen, Raaghav... This is no time to fall in love and lose track of more important things in life. I need eight years to settle down and there is no place for love in this period."

"We can still talk to each other?" he suggested

"No, we can't. No talking at all."

"I love you." I knew too well what he was trying to do. He wanted me to say it too. And I was fighting like a warrior against it.

"Please, don't force me to say it."

"I wish I could. Not saying that you love me, is it another sacrifice that you're making for Aunty?"

"No, it's for me. It's for my sanity... For staying alive without you," I answered softly.

"You don't need to stay alive without me..." he began again.

I tried turning away, exasperated a little for him not being able to understand my situation.

"Okay, I'm sorry... I understand. But you can at least write it." He pushed forward his big hand under my nose. I looked up at him, confused. He pulled out the sketch pens from my other hand and pointed them at his out stretched hand.

"Write it," he insisted, attempting to smile. "Just one last time, please."

I sighed, unable to fight off his silly, yet adorable request. I wanted to shout at him, pull him into a hug and squeeze the life out of him, kiss him like crazy, marry and run away with him. But all I did was snatch the sketch pens and fill up his hand. I did the best I could, venting my emotions out into my drawing – a big 'I Love you, Raaghav' in the centre, signed off with the date, while little ILU's adorned each of the three phalanges in a finger. Staring at it for a good complete minute, I looked up to find him gazing at me.

"Now, I won't wash this hand for the next eight years."

I couldn't help but fall into his attempts to make me smile.

He moved forward as if wanting to hug. I took a step back. He stopped immediately.

"I can't Raaghav. I'm sorry. Please forgive me." I took another step away.

"Forgive me, Ira. I can't stop loving you."

I turned away as the dam broke and warm tears flowed freely over my cheeks. The metro had just arrived and I walked into the crowd, hoping to lose him in all the rush. It was tough fighting against the de-boarding crowd but I managed to enter the metro and the doors closed just behind me. I looked back to see him standing on the platform helplessly.

I love you, Raaghav, I mouthed, as the metro started moving.

Unable to face Mom's cold behaviour, I moved into my Bua's place. It was close to college and exams were approaching so it would help me save travel time and devote myself thoroughly to studies. At least, these were the reasons enough to convince Dad.

Once at Bua's place, I bunked college a lot, exams being the last thing on my mind. In reality, I feared facing Raaghav.

Thankfully, the preparatory leave was declared soon and I became the voluntary victim of solitude in my allotted room. Unfortunately or fortunately though, the less I saw of Raaghav, the more he started to become ingrained into my thoughts. He kept his promise of not calling me up, but messaged daily. I didn't read a single one, rather deleted them all together at night. Even though unread and deleted, they would haunt me and I'd occasionally wake up in the middle of the night – dreadfully lost and lonely. On nights like these, I would pull out my beloved collection of Raaghav's annual day snaps and cry like a maniac.

For the first one month or so the nightmare with Mom had me numbed and all that my heart could do was shiver in fear and regret. My brain managed to open up for the exams that filled up the second month without Raaghav. The third month saw reconciliation between my brain and my heart.

Well, sort of.

Brain – Falling in love with Raaghav was my biggest mistake.

Heart – Breaking up with him was the worst decision I could have taken.

Brain – I shouldn't have given wings to my infatuation for him.

Heart – But what is wrong in loving?

Brain – There is an age and a time to fall in love. And you just can't go ahead and get physical with any guy whom you think is right.

Heart – Raaghav is not just any guy. He is different.

Brain – What makes him different? He doesn't even accept me as his girlfriend in college.

Heart – That's what makes him different. There are guys who claim to be with me just because I've smiled at them. That's how cheap guys are. Raaghav knows I love him, still he does not show off before the world.

Brain – But he can at least talk normally in college? What is wrong in that?

Heart – I don't know. All I know is that I love him...

Brain – Love does not exist in today's world. It was a thing of the ancient times. Where have I last seen true, happy love around me?

Heart – In Raaghav's eyes for me...

Brain – Raaghav's eyes! Yes, they are the culprit behind all this. They are the reason for which I brought shame upon Mom.

Heart – Mom doesn't understand me at all. She is too obsessed with society to see her own daughter for real. She thinks I'm a fool. But I'm not. I trust Raaghav, he would never use me.

Brain – He has never used me in fact. I have been after him since the beginning and now I am the one who has left him in the middle of nowhere.

Heart – Why does Mom's perspective matter suddenly? Why does her view point matter at all?

Brain – Because she's my mom?

Heart – So what? This is a stupid reason. She didn't even give me a chance to explain my feelings...

Brain – Our patriarchal society does not have place for such feelings. I am a girl. I should be all shush about my emotions. I don't have the right to be open about my feelings, to pursue the guy I like, to get physical before marriage.

To hell with what the society thinks! Tired with the battle that had just raged within me, I plonked onto the bed, toppling over the toys scattered on it.

I sighed. Both mind and heart had gone silent again and I robotically began picking up the toys. As I arranged them meticulously on the bed, I envied my kid brother, Kavin. How easy it was to be kids. No worries, no conflicts, no mind-heart wars... Everything was simple. I picked up a big brown teddy bear, the last to be fallen on the floor and turned it to face me, only to be taken aback. A hazy memory hidden under layers and layers of growing up got uncovered and standing before me in the room was me, all of four years old, reciting a poem.

'Jack and Jill went up the hill
To fetch a pail of water
Jack fell down and broke his crown
And Jill came tumbling after'

I had imagined being Jill. Deeply in love with my Jack – a huge brown teddy bear that I had been gifted on my 1ˢᵗ birthday. Jack was soft and fluffy, and huggable and warm and had a beautiful smile. Of all the dolls that I had, I loved only him.

Every day, I would make a big pile on the corner of my bed with all the blankets and pillows that I could find in the house. Then, with Jack under my arm, I would climb over my soft yet treacherous cliff singing the rhyme again and again. Once at the top, I would spend hours with Jack. Talking, playing, dancing – sometimes hugging him to sleep. And then at the end of my play I would tumble down with Jack with the delight that only a young child can truly celebrate. Eventually I grew up but Jack and Jill always remained my favourite love story.

I blinked fiercely as I came back to the present – my Jack, the first love of my life, my big brown teddy bear had green eyes.

Slowly, an uncanny realization was dawning upon me. Of all my dolls, my favourite had been a bear! I had never been a normal girl. I am *not* the typical girl the world expects me to be. I am not what Mom expects me to be.

Suddenly, something got over me and I realized I had made the wrong choice. I should have chosen Raaghav when I actually fell for Mom's advice – no matter how imposed it was.

Yes! It made sense now! I was in a fix because my heart was not convinced of my decision. I had to give myself a chance. I had to give my relation with Raaghav a chance. At least then, it would be my fault if something went wrong and no one else would be required to blame. I wouldn't hold anyone else responsible for my state then. This is exactly what I needed to do to feel at peace at again.

But how? I hadn't interacted with Raaghav for the last three months. I just couldn't suddenly call him up. How would I begin? What would I say?

And then it struck it me.

The IDA fest was coming up next week – a two day fest in which colleges from all over participated in various competitions like dancing, singing, arts, quizzes and the stuff. Our college too was participating in many of the events. But the one that was of interest to me was the Fashion Show. Raaghav was coordinating it.

The preparations had begun last month and participant selection had completed three weeks ago. Rehearsals had been on in full swing, as I would occasionally catch the group practising in the corridors. I just had to join the team somehow and Manvi was my only hope.

One sign had been enough to push me, to ignite a spark within me, but not enough to go up straight and talk to him. The show had come across as an opportunity. I was hoping for some more signs to strengthen my belief of being destined for Raaghav.

Only, I was hoping too little.

Manvi ran up to me, jumping with excitement, as I cautiously entered the practice hall next day. I had called her the night before, enquiring whether there was any need for help in the backstage team.

"You've got a role in the show!" she whispered into my ear.

I stood confused, my face blank.

"Someone backed out today morning and the lady devil's walk is all yours now!"

I looked across the room towards the music system where Raaghav was busy with some other guys – jamming the record for the show. Our eyes met for just a second but I knew it instantly. He had done it for me – putting me in the show was impossible at this time, but he had. How, I had no clue, but he look on his face was enough to make me sure. With the show just round the corner, this kind of an addition on the team was utterly unexpected. And the blatant openness on Raaghav's part on the whole scenario was like a bolt out of the blue. I became the talk of the college in merely one hour – the girl who Raaghav had selected.

The entire team noticed the vibes between us – while they'd call it a connection, only the two of us knew it was tension. I had simply rushed and given in to my intuition but was this really the correct thing to do?

There was another big issue that I had to handle. The fest was being held in Ludhiana and there had been a long discussion among us friends, about two weeks ago – we'd all go together as a group or no one would go at all. Ultimately it was my adamant refusal that had the entire group opt out. Not getting permission from Dad was my apparent sole reason, though in honesty – the reason for not going was Raaghav.

Now suddenly, the reason *for going* was Raaghav again – but this time, I had messed up. I couldn't tell them the truth and there was nothing I could lie about either. This time the decision was complicated – I had to choose between my friends and my love; a harshly splitting choice.

I lost my friends for good.

Disowned and disoriented, I loitered around the creative girls group, who accepted me gladly.

Convincing Dad in allowing me to go for the fest was a nightmare. His daughter participating in a fashion show turned out to be the most infuriating request ever. World War Three ensued in our little flat and much damage later, I emerged as the winner. I was participating in the fashion show and going to Ludhiana.

Little idea did I have that my life was going to change, forever.

⌘

Present day...

The room wasn't big, just good enough for five-six of us.

It had a bed on one side, which was being hijacked by the girls from all sides and a little couch on the other. I put down my bag and went over to the window, pulling away the blinds. I turned to find Raaghav standing at the door – looking huge against its little frame.

"The bus leaves for the venue at ten in the morning," he announced to no one in particular.

I sighed as he left – for right or for wrong, I was here.

Reminiscing during the entire journey from the beginning had been enjoyable but exhausting too – I felt fatigued. Not to forget, anxious and overwhelmed. It was the first time in my life that I was out of home, on a trip with friends – more specifically, out on a trip with Raaghav. I knew something would happen on this trip. Either it was this way or that. And I had taken my chances. Whatever the outcome, I would be sure of having tried for once – of giving destiny a chance. I stood in the shower till all the hot water ran out. Packing my hair in one towel and myself in another, I opened the door.

Only, to shut it back again. Outside, in the room, sitting on the couch was none other than Raaghav. He was bent over some papers, discussing something with Simar and Anjali.

Thank God, he hadn't seen me! I took a few deep breaths to calm down my pacing heart before calling out to Manvi. Answering almost immediately, she handed me my clothes.

The universe had presented me with quite a few signs – Jack the teddy bear coming back to memory out of the blue, getting a role into the show at the last minute, Dad agreeing to send me off, the green lenses showing up, the sign board with Raaghav's wordings, the hand painting... Phew!

But how was I to go and talk to Raaghav. What irony. I had been crazily after him for the last one year, and now suddenly I couldn't go up and talk to him.

Maybe I was losing my mind completely. I poured myself a glass of water before settling into the bed, lost in my own thoughts. I wondered whether Raaghav would come up and talk to me. Could Raaghav do that? He had put on such a firm mask for so long before all these people here. Would he suddenly uncover it all?

I sighed, knowing that would never happen. No matter how much I wished for it.

Maybe love wasn't so easy to fall in as I had taken it to be. Maybe each love story had to come with a set of problems and hardships – ours being this distance I had put us in.

I tossed aside the elaborate props that had been crafted for most of the participants, ranging from painted boots to coloured nail extensions, fairy wands and cursing sticks, the joker's hat and the elves pointed ears – we had it all. Of them all, two were my favourite. In the entire 'Angels and Demons' themed fashion show of ours, only two participants were donning wings – one an angel, the other a devil.

Raaghav was the angel, while I was the devil – perfectly apt.

I looked up. He was on the phone, calling someone over to the room. He had his own room but he preferred to stay here. He looked up from the sheets and I went back to the wings. Students came and went as he finalized and cross checked the events for tomorrow – tiny details were discussed, last minute changes handled and inadvertent problems solved. I heard it all – one ear permanently pined at the couch. Three and a half hours later, Manvi and I finally finished the last piece of the halo – each of the angels was wearing one.

Dinner had been ordered for the lot of people in the small room. I looked around the dozen or so faces around me, shying away from the one I loved. None of us slept. It was a fun night. Someone put on the speakers into a phone and soon everyone was dancing – everyone except for me and Raaghav.

He was laid back on the couch while I was sitting on the bed and the others were dancing between the two of us – crazy, stupid dancing. I laughed and amidst the gyrating bodies, I caught Raaghav gazing at me, a soft smile on his beautiful face. Reluctantly almost, with one final look at me, he got up and left the room.

I was once again left alone in the crowd around me.

"Yipppeeeee, yay, yay!"

I closed my ears with my hands as most of the team shouted into the air. The fashion show had been a great success!

Although the results were to be announced the next day, the team was overjoyed, now outside the building – hooting, laughing, and congratulating each other. It was time for snaps and pictures.

The photographer was a typical over the board professional, much at ease with a young crowd. Taking advantage of the casual attitude of most of the students, he had them strike close and overtly expressive poses. Not that anyone seemed to mind.

Angels and demons would never have teamed up the way they did today, with friends hugging and couples feigning kisses. Before I knew it, it was me and Him before the camera. We posed soberly, not looking at each other. The photographer had other plans though.

"Ah, such a sexy couple!" He didn't shy one bit in exclaiming out loud. Another sign, I mused within.

"One an angel, pure and sublime like heaven itself," he walked around Raaghav, creasing out his gown. "And the other a hot devil, black magic that even hell cannot resist," he dramatized, straightening my falling X-ray wings.

I just managed to see Raaghav's face tighten. It was easy to know he did not like the way the photographer was dancing around me.

"I'll do it." He looked curtly at him and inching closer, creased open my sagging wings. I didn't dare look into his face.

"Perfect!" beamed the photographer.

"What a pair! Now look into each other's eyes, as if the devil has fallen in love with the angel – hell in love with heaven," he declared in rising tempo.

That did it all. Whether the expression came or not, was left for the zealous photographer to decide, but what surely came was a storm. A storm of emotions threatening to burst me from within rose like a tornado – fiery and wild. As some whispering angles standing nearby joined in for group snaps, I took the opportunity and ran away.

Dashing away from all the commotion, I reached the dressing room behind the stage, panting slightly.

It was dimly lit, the colourful stage lights from the adjacent tent swirling around at intervals. Carefully avoiding the mess scattered on the floor, I walked up to the very extreme wall of the cold room. I stared at my image in the little mirror before me. I couldn't recognize the face. What had I become?

I felt so distant – hiding myself under layers and layers of pretence. Deep within, I was feeling sad and lonely. For once I was expecting Raaghav to come up and talk to me, but it wasn't happening. I had left everything to destiny by coming along on this trip. If Raaghav would come up and talk to me, I'd forget everything in the world and become his. Else, I'd forget him for good and forever. I shut my eyes tight, seeing the chances of the latter increasing manifold. My whole belief in the signs around me was falling to the ground, tumbled over by the harsh truth of reality – this plan hadn't turned out to be as easy as I had imagined it to be. I could now see tiny, colourful streaks in the darkness of my shut eyes when suddenly I heard a voice behind me.

"Congratulations."

I turned around with a jerk and froze.

Raaghav was standing at the door.

There was light behind him, giving a surreal glow to his silhouette. He looked taller than usual. The stage lights passed over him, illuminating the cuts of his face and throwing sparkle into his eyes.

Once again, I was mesmerized by an angel – calm and quiet, he stood in his white gown. Only this time he really had his wings and halo on. His green eyes had caught mine like a magnet and they refused to let go. Not that I wanted to.

For all the life in my soul, I wanted to hold on to the moment. I stood there, staring into the green gems, memories flooding my head.

Memories of stalking him in corridors, teasing him, trying to capture him in my phone, stealing his snaps from the office, waiting for him at the metro.

Memories of park swings and bowling games, of Chinese vans and metro lines, of flowers and gifts and platform lifts.

Memories of evenings spent walking hand in hand and nights spent talking till dawn.

Memories of our dates, hugs and kisses.

Memories of us together, happily lost in love.

A tear rolled down my cheek and I turned away.

"Ira," he walked upto me, stopping just behind, making sure not to touch me.

I closed my eyes.

"Ira, I love you. Please come back to me. Please." He paused, and I could hear him sigh.

"Ira, I don't want to put any pressure on you. I value your decisions. I respect your promises to your mom. But please don't shut me out. We can be friends at least. I promise I'll never make you feel uncomfortable...." his voice trailed off, just as a tear trailed down my cheek.

"You have never made me feel uncomfortable, Raaghav," I whispered softly, my back still towards him.

And maybe my speaking out gave him more courage.

He inched closer and gently holding an elbow, turned me around to face him. I couldn't resist. I didn't want to anymore. Slowly, I turned to look up into his eyes. My heart sank as I realized they were filled with tears, and I lost control over my own. As the salty streams trickled down my eyes, he cupped my face in his warm, soft hands. And as if on cue, the commentator outside stopped his gibberish announcements and suddenly the song started playing – our song.

All signs and signals summed up into one moment of realization. I had not for a moment been wrong in falling for this guy before me. He was my only love, my reason of existence, my purpose of living – my Raaghav, my destiny. All of Mom's fears, apprehensions and tensions had wrongly displaced the true feelings I had for him. My conviction in loving him had been right all along. I had lost not when Mom had found out about us, but when I had allowed her to steer away my true emotions for him. It was only now that I was realizing completely the extreme fault in her conjecture.

Raaghav and I, we were not just another couple.

We were special. The love that we had between us was special. It wasn't only love. It was much more – the love that you rise up for, rather than falling in. The love that did not need to be burdened with problems and struggles – it had come along smoothly, just because it was meant to be so – pure, easy and full of life.

The realization struck like a flash of lightning across the clouds of doubt – clear, sharp and instant. And with complete acceptance of my destiny – giving up all pretence, I broke free of the chains that had been limiting me and surrendered myself to him. Enwrapping him below his wings, I burst out completely. I burrowed myself into his chest, letting out all the agony that I had been carrying around. Losing all sense, I cried and cried and cried.

He held me firmly, one hand across my waist as if he would never let go. With the other he caressed my hair, kissing my head over and over again. Holding onto each other, we stood there as our song played till the very end.

As the room filled with silence, he gently lifted my head with two fingers. My face was wet with all the crying and my hair was all tangled. He tucked back my hair with one hand, while taking out a handkerchief from his gown. I couldn't help but let out a little laugh. He always had a handkerchief on him, even when he was wrapped in a gown. He sighed with relief and a smile brightened up his face.

I let go off him, thinking the handkerchief was for me. But he firmly pulled me back into his embrace, guiding my hands over his waist.

"Let them stay here," he said softly.

Holding me tightly in one arm, he wiped away my tears.

"I feel my heart beating when I see you smile and laugh. But when you cry..." He wiped a fresh tear from the corner of my eye, only this time he used his lips instead of the handkerchief. "It takes my life away."

I closed my eyes.

"All of this that you are going through for me, for us... Please, let me be a part of it."

"Took you long enough to say it!" I quipped.

"You made me promise never to call you up again, yet I messaged you daily! How else was I supposed to say it?" he asked, obviously taken aback at my retort.

"I didn't read a single one of them..." I mumbled sheepishly, toying with the cross on his long pearl necklace.

He sighed and smiled.

Cupping back my face, he planted another kiss on the bridge of my nose. "It doesn't matter. Nothing matters now that you are here with me. I love you, Ira. I'm ready for whatever you want. You want eight years to be settled, I'm ready for it...

But let it be eight years for us and not you alone. Be with me in those eight years. I'll give you whatever you ask of me, but please don't ask me to leave you."

The look in his eyes was tearing me apart.

It didn't take me a second to give him an answer.

"Your love is all I need, Raaghav," I whispered silently into his lips, lingering inches away from mine.

He sighed deeply, pulling me even closer.

"You'll never have less of it, Ira. Trust me."

"I do," I replied.

I slowly wiped away the precious drop as he gazed upon my face, a soft smile on his face – one that I could look at forever, yet I had not seen for the last three months.

"Please, don't ever leave me again, Ira. I can't live without you."

I buried back my head into his chest, deeply breathing in his lovely scent, as he hugged me tight. All the sadness, all the regret, all the frustration – all negativity had dissipated.

There was absolutely no place on earth I'd rather be than this little circle between his warm embrace.

I felt complete, content and happy.

We were together and that was all I needed to be alive and happy – forever and ever.

We didn't win the fashion show, but I won what was going to be the biggest win in my life. Not many of the students were in the best of spirits and only a few were keen to visit the remaining spots on our short trip – an ISKCON temple and the Golden Temple.

Raaghav and I were amongst the few.

All the way to the ISKCON temple, Anjali kept searching for fresh fruits in order to offer the deities but to no avail. We finally ended up buying a dozen pastries before entering the sweet little hall. It was hardly a room, but the deities were adorable. As I stood gazing into their beautiful eyes, I did not realize when Raaghav had sneaked up behind me. Just at the same time, the priest appeared before us.

With one look at the two of us, he went back to the deities and picked up a large flower garland right off the lord. Adding to it a covered bowl he came forward and handed it to us, our hands outstretched together.

As we bowed to collect the prasad, he blessed us, "Stay blessed and happily married forever."

Whoa! That came as the biggest sign I could have imagined. It was as if my Lord standing before me had already sanctioned us as a couple.

I turned towards Raaghav's face, only to find him gleaming with satisfaction.

"I told you! You are mine and only mine."

My happiness knew no bounds as we boarded the bus.

It hadn't taken long for the universe to seal my fate. The bold step that I had taken in coming back to Raaghav had been certified by divinity's own blessings.

Grinning like a crazy child, I handed over the prasad to Anjali. She grinned back with equal excitement as she uncovered the bowl – it was full of fresh fruits.

Wishes were becoming true all around and all in good time!

The journey back to Delhi turned out to be revealing in ways more than one.

Raaghav no longer seemed to mind everyone talking about us. He was so open about being with me to the extent that he actually reserved a couple seat for us on the bus. This was surprisingly new and refreshing. I was basking in the new found freedom of expression that he had developed –not shying away from an audience, laughing off the teasing in good spirit and not leaving my side for one minute.

Most of our talks were were catching up about the last three months. I was wildly surprised at Raaghav's upfront nature with his family. He had gone forth and told his parents about me – about our commitment to each other to be specific.

"I just wanted them to know I had made up my mind. Eight years you had asked me to wait," he said, rolling his eyes in feigned exasperation.

We sat gazing into each other's eyes letting our hearts do the talking. Tucked up comfortably in one blanket, he moved in to adjust the window curtain. Only he never got the chance to go back. Turning his face towards me he planted a small kiss on my dry lips. Warm and wet, he tasted delicious. He lingered before my face, his breathing becoming one with mine. His hand moved down from the curtains to my waist, cupping it warmly, his thumb just resting against the base of my breast.

Sweet pangs of delight spread across my body as his fingers caressed me slightly, and he kissed me again. This time not letting go. I held his face in my arms, responding to his rhythm – slowly, leisurely, blissfully.

We were together again. And this time nothing could do us apart. Softly embraced in the moment of finding back lost love, we kissed under the blanket of the night.

We reached Amritsar at four a.m. – early morning for many, but late night as per the definition of the young adults in the bus. Just a handful of us, namely Simar, Anjali, Manvi, Devi, Raaghav and I made our way onto the chilly tiles of the Golden Temple.

As we walked into the main shrine, little was I aware that another memory was adding up to my already eventful love story. The place was oozing with serene sacredness, and Raaghav held my hand as we circumambulated and bowed together before the holy Granth.

Surprising me, and more so the group of girls with us, he didn't leave my hand at all. Simar winked at me as we walked over to the sacred pond, secretly sending fly kisses to me behind his back. Feeling blessed beyond measured I dipped my hands into the sacred pond, turning around to meet another magical sight. Raaghav, standing with his hands folded in prayer, eyes closed and head bowed was turning a golden tint in the rays of the rising sun.

The sight was as precious as it could get, making me realize once again that Raaghav was a gift sent by the heavens to me. I seeped in all details, closing my eyes, imprinting it to memory – one that I would recall with gratitude over the years to come.

My decision was stamped yet again.

The irrational fears implanted in my mind by Mom had disappeared completely and all that was left was a scar – a distant relation with my mother. Overjoyed at having Raaghav back in life, I made no attempt whatsoever to reach out to her. I didn't even ask for my diary. Shutting her out was probably the easiest I could do and it wasn't long before the bond fizzled out. Eventually, it didn't matter having her around and I shifted back to my place, not in the least worried about her. I had better things to think about – my upcoming first anniversary with Raaghav, for instance.

The 7th of February. The day stood so fresh and vivid in memory. The day when Mr President had walked into our class, looking for fresh executives. The day when one 'congratulations' from him won me the purpose of my existence. I knew just the right thing to do.

I took a day off from college for the elaborate plan that I had up my sleeve. First, I had to lie to Raaghav. I messaged him early morning that I wasn't well and wouldn't be able to make it to college much to his disappointment.

Once he was hooked, I quickly dressed up and left home, picking up the bag I had carefully packed. No one at home knew I wasn't going to college and I kept it that way. Soon enough I was on my way to the nearest Archies outlet. Smiling at the boy behind the counter, I handed him the balance money for the shopping I had done at their store a week ago. I quickly glanced though the three big bags he had readied for me. All the stuff seemed to be in there. Thanking him, I made my way to the next stop – a little florist at the end of the market. Choosing among my favourite, I selected the best flowers and got the fresh stems packed in newspaper. Once done, I merrily skipped along to the mall nearby, humming my favourite song at the moment – 'Criminal' by Britney Spears.

Mama, I'm in love with a criminal and this kind of love isn't rational, it's physical

Mama, please don't cry, I will be alright, all reasons aside I just can't deny, I love this guy.

It resonated aptly with my scenario. I entered the washroom inside the mall and opened my bag, keeping aside all my goodies. Folded neatly inside was my black sari from the school farewell. It was a shimmery georgette piece, embellished with golden thread in self. I took off my shirt and packed it into the bag. The blouse for the sari I had already worn. Quickly pulling down the petticoat, I wrapped the sari neatly over myself. The next step was to do some really good make up and look older. This was difficult. I wasn't very good with plastering up my face and it took me a little while to get things in place. Finally, letting my hair fall open, I put on the heels that I had carried along and stuffed back all my other things into the bag. With one last check at myself, I walked out of the mall, hoping every bit that I looked older. Hiring an auto, I moved on to my final destination – the hotel nearby.

This was going to be the most difficult part of all, or so I thought. I headed over to the reception, faking an aura of superiority and professionalism. Confidence had never been an issue for me, and I as requested a room for the day, the concierge seemed all fine. Ten minutes later, done with the formalities and payments, I was led to my room by a young lady, wishing me a lovely evening.

"I'm sure going to have one!" I smiled at her, for reasons she couldn't have imagined in the wildest of her dreams. Locking the door from inside, I quickly unwrapped the sari, getting rid of all accessories with it. I thoroughly washed my face, glad to be rid of all the makeup. I hadn't been too sure of my plan without a grown up look. Booking a room in such a big hotel, walking in as a casual college student and having Raaghav over seemed all too suspicious and hence I had thrown in the sari and the professional attitude. No one would doubt a working woman for taking a break from her meeting schedule. So, I hoped.

Comfortably back in my shirt and jeans, I jumped straight into setting up the room. Glancing at the clock, I realized I didn't have too much time. Quickly, I busied myself into bringing to life the picture that I had imagined for today – pouring my heart and soul into it. Surprisingly, my phone didn't ring once, as if God didn't want me to be disturbed. About an hour later I looked around. Smiling at my artwork, I cleaned up the little mess around me. There! The stage was set – the room was ready to celebrate our first anniversary.

I picked up my phone and texted Raaghav.

Waiting for your call.

Love you.

I settled onto the couch and laid back my head, thinking about how things had changed between us since Ludhiana. We were connected deeper after the three month long separation and it felt that the distance had ignited a certain kind of fever within. A fever that had my body craving for a medicine, and that medicine was Raaghav. As I thought about it, I could feel warmth spreading all over me. And suddenly the phone rang. It was Him. I cancelled the call, quickly typing in a message.

Do you trust me?

I received a reply immediately.

With my life.

I smiled, typing in the next message, choosing my words carefully.

Then could you do something for me, without asking any questions?

Again, an instant reply.

With pleasure, Ira.

He wasn't asking any questions. My heart said he already knew I was up to something. After all, I had never been able to hide things from him. It didn't matter. He'd never guess something this big! I typed in the set of instructions I had to give him and hit send.

Come over to Hotel Jade Nest and walk straight in to Room No 307. In case they ask at the reception, just tell them you're here for a client discussion. Message me once you reach the building. Love you loads. Mmmmmuuuaah!

I took in a deep breath, trying to calm my pacing heart. I was nervous, but not more than I was excited. He didn't reply. I didn't call either. I wanted his anticipation to be as high as mine and there was no better way than teasing around. Passing time became punishing. I sat on the edge of the couch, staring intently at my phone waiting for his message. After what seemed like eternity, the bell to my room rang, making me jump up in surprise. I ran over, peeking through the spy hole. It was Raaghav.

My heart pounding like a train on fire, I swept my back and wet my lips for the millionth time, before opening the door.

"Hey!" I cooed softly, allowing him in but stopping him in the gallery itself.

The look on his face was a complete mess – joy and fear everything stirred up on his beautiful face, with a big question mark in the centre. I giggled, taking his bag and dropping it to the ground. Pulling my arms over his shoulders, I looked deep into his eyes and stepped onto his feet – one foot at a time, ending all space between us. He clasped me firmly from my waist, bending down to kiss me. I kissed him back, relishing the heat from his body. And as our lips parted, I softly whispered in his ears.

"Happy Anniversary, Raaghav."

The look on his face changed into one of surprise and he smiled beautifully.

"Of course! Happy Anniversary, Ira. The 7th of Feb, how could I not remember? The day you had been selected for the college committee!"

It filled up my heart with warm emotion to know that he remembered. He pulled me tighter, planting soft kisses all over my face and sticking to my lips with the last one, before looking up.

"Walk," I whispered as I saw him looking around, laying my head onto his chest.

With me on his feet, hanging onto his shoulders, he walked slowly towards the bed. I pulled up a switch as we crossed the points in the gallery, not letting go of him yet. The room got softly flooded with lights and he paused. I turned up to face him. His lips parted slightly, his eyes moist, his face glowing – he stood dumbstruck.

Kissing him softly, I uttered the three simple words again.

"I love you."

He looked around the room, completely dazed. My eyes followed his as they moved across, starting from one corner.

Near the bedside table, on our left, I had propped up three small cards, each with a pink rose leaning against it. Behind the cards was a bigger card and supporting it was a bunch of yellow tulips. The bed, finely made and undisturbed, I had covered with red rose petals. Another side table on the other side of the bed had the same pattern of cards. The roses on that side were yellow, while the tulips were purple. On the far end of the room, right beside the curtains was a table that I had stocked up with ten gifts of varying sizes, brightly wrapped in golden and red. On either side of the gifts was a bunch of carnations. The mirror on the wall opposite the bed had multiple hearts of varying sizes taped in concentric circles. Standing close to us on our right, was a tall lamp, around which I had twirled some ribbons and hung little heart danglers. A big heart cushion was taped on the lamp shade while heart shaped balloons were scattered all over the floor. Finally, the bed was bordered with lavender perfumed candles that now had the room smelling heavenly sweet.

I looked back at him, trying to assess his reaction, hoping he had liked my efforts.

He looked down at me, still dazed – expressionless.

He looked back over the room, and then again at me, slowly shaking his head.

"You didn't like it?" I asked in a small voice, my smile lost.

"Like it?" he almost squealed, with a spark in his eyes!

"Ira, all of this..." He waved a hand around the room, shaking his head as if in disbelief. "It's unbelievable."

He paused, taking his time to get the right words. He was smilingly now.

"Ira, this is more than I can ever thank you for. I can't believe you did all this for me," he said softly, looking into my eyes.

"I love you, Raaghav," I whispered as if it were an explanation.

"I know, sweetheart. I never thought a girl could do so much for a guy... This is so beautiful... And so full of love...But then you are you..." his voice faded as he buried his face into my hair, inhaling deeply.

He sighed deeply pulling me into a tighter embrace. Carrying me on his feet, he walked over to the couch, where he settled down, careful not to hurt me. He sat with his legs apart, cradling me like a baby.

He wanted to speak, I knew it. These were the moments I so craved for; Raaghav baring his heart before me.

"Ira, I can never explain what you mean to me," he started softly. "I realized how much I love you when I lost you. Those three months... You shut me out completely and I got scared. What if you never came back? What if you got over me? I went crazy fretting over it."

He paused, teary-eyed. I immediately pulled up his face, kissing each of the closed eye lids.

"I cried... I cried a lot, until one day, I thought I just couldn't take it anymore. I thought it was all over and I had lost you forever. That day, I went to a temple. I wanted answers. I wanted to fight God. But all I could do was cry. And pray to have you back. I prayed to get my Ira back."

He paused, gazing across my face.

"And he listened to me! The very next week you showed up for the IDA fest. How was I not to let you on the show?!"

We both laughed softly.

"God had sent you for me. Not just that day for the show. He sent you to JCDS for me. He sent you to earth for me."

Pulling me closer, he planted a big kiss on my hairline, lingering there for a few seconds.

"I love you Ira, and I'll never be able to explain how much. But I love you. I love you so much that I want to spend every moment of my life with you. I want to live life with you. I want to travel the world with you. I want to make you happy and hug you to sleep every night. And I want to wake up to kiss you..." he kissed me softly on my parted lips before continuing. "... like this, every morning when I wake up. I want to be with you through all your dreams, your fights, your ups and downs. And I want to share all of mine with you. I want to become one with you, Ira. Not just for this life, but forever."

Both his hands cupping my face, our foreheads touching each other, he whispered into my face, "I love you, Ira. I love you."

I closed my eyes, a stream of salty water trickling down my cheeks onto his thumbs. I sighed. I couldn't remember when I had felt so precious, so loved before in my life. He had simply taken my heart away, all over again.

I snuggled up into his chest, kissing the place over his heart.

"I love you, Raaghav." was all I could manage to say.

He hugged me tight, burrowing his face into my hair and we sat there.

"Come, I want to read the cards," he whispered into my hair. I gladly got up, guiding him to the side table.

They were not merely words, but were parts of my heart that I was gifting to him... along with all of me.

Like doves in love that wander in the sky
Fly with me as the years go by...
Like the waves merge together in every low and high
Rise with me as the years go by...

Like the raindrops splatter when the clouds heave a sigh
Fall with me as the years go by...
Like the colors of the rainbow into each other tie
Let you and I be we as the years go by...

Like the golden rays kiss the sun goodbye
Shine with me as the years go by...
Like the winds whisper of a truth and a lie,
Share with me as the years go by...

Like the joy that hides in the sparkle of an eye
Smile with me as the years go by...
Like the stars that twinkle even after they die
Live with me as the years go by...

Raaghav's precious green eyes were glistening beautifully.

— *I always thought true love is hard to find. Lucky I am, the stars brought you to me*

True to heart I'm yours forever, as true and as forever as love can be

— *Lost in the world, I believed love comes with many a trial and tribulation*

Now finding myself in your arms, I'm glad mine has been a warm celebration

— *I've never felt more blessed; having you near, your hand in mine*

As we walk together on the journey ahead, our love is bound to shine

— *And though seasons of all colors will come across to us in time*

You'll forever remain my beloved intoxication; sweet, pure and sublime.

⌘

I could feel him drinking in the words. Hundreds of kisses and love-yous later, we reached the table of gifts. He asked why I had given him ten gifts, something which I really wanted him to ask. Because 1+0 equals 1 and it was our 1st anniversary I had quipped gleefully, taken aback by his hearty laughter at my response. Hugging me into his bear arms, he had planted ten kisses on my nose declaring I was a kid.

He turned out to be an even younger kid than me when it came to opening the gifts. Excited beyond measure, he enjoyed opening up each wrapping as I sat beside him, supervising his act. A wallet, a key chain, a pair of handkerchiefs with his initials, a tie set, a mug, a photo frame, a pen, a personal planner and an album containing my snaps – he loved them all, the album the most.

The tenth gift, a small box, I deferred him from opening it till later.

Hunger was crawling over us and it was time to satiate our bellies. We had lunch on the couch while the bed retained its pristine glory. All through our rajma chawal celebration, he asked me how I had managed to pull this off – the gifts, the cards, the room booking and the money to do it all? And as I told him everything in detail he wasn't only amazed, he was bowled over by it. Especially by the part where I told him about my sari act.

"So, you came here in a saree, huh?" he asked, raising an eyebrow, putting away the lunch boxes.

I nodded, smiling knowingly. He loved to see me in a sari. He would say it all too often. He would remember the Fresher's day image of mine and fantasize over it.

"You should have kept it on," he said teasingly.

"Really?" I asked tentatively, moving one leg across him. Holding him by his shoulders, I climbed onto his lap, straddling him like a horse. I was sure he was imagining me in a sari now and I knew the effect it had on him.

He rested back his head, gazing at me above him; a sparkle in his eyes, a smile on his lips.

"Really... This shirt is boring," he said.

"I can take it off," I whispered into his lips, kissing them softly. He responded, one hand cupping my face while the other holding me by my back. I could feel the warmth of his hand through my zipper.

We kissed ardently till I broke off, leaving him breathing deeply. He moved in trying to kiss me again, pulling me closer into himself. I could feel a desire in his pull, a longing in his green eyes. We kissed again.

I slowly unbuttoned his shirt, running my hand across his chest. He looked deep into my eyes before closing his, kissing my forehead softly.

"I love you, Ira," he whispered, his struggle to stop himself apparent on his face.

I suddenly remembered his rule of no sex before marriage. But today I had vowed to break it. I turned towards the table and grabbed the last gift, placing it in his hands.

"The last gift."

He relaxed as the moment passed away and carefully unwrapped the little box. Inside was a small placard, and he sighed softly as he read it. On it, as beautifully that I could, I had written one word – ME. He looked up and before he could say a word, I placed a finger on his lips, shushing him.

"I'm yours. All yours... For life and after."

Removing the finger, I planted a soft kiss on his lips.

"I love you, Raaghav. There's nothing I fear. I'm yours and you're mine," I whispered, kissing him, fervently this time, not letting go.

"Make love to me, Raaghav." I didn't stop kissing. "Please."

He kissed me back with a heightened response. My hands were all over his bare chest, feeling him like never before. His hands had slid into my shirt and onto my back. The feeling of his warm hands on my skin was always a pleasure. Stirring me up from inside, it had the power to make me want him. As his hands moved forwards, caressing gently across my waist, I let go of his lips, pulling my head back. His kisses followed the curve of my outstretched neck all the way down to where my zipper began. He grabbed the zip between his lips, gently touching my skin where it lay, spreading pangs of delight across my body. Slowly, he started pulling down the zipper, breathing softly as he went lower.

My fingers were entwined in his soft hair and with each warm breath that fell on my skin, I felt myself pulling him closer. He paused right between the hills, burying his face deep into the valley. His thumbs had sneaked up into the lower strap of my bra and were now caressing the hill bases while he gently planted kisses all over the revealed slopes. While every kissed spot seemed to be melting under the heat of passion, the peaks had hardened.

I was quivering with delight, aching with desire and I wrapped my legs tighter around him as I felt him rise below me. With one hand cupped across the nape of my neck and the other firmly supporting my hips, he carried me over to the rose covered bed.

The room around me was becoming a blur as the magic of love was given wings.

The passion grew and covered us in sweaty drops of nectar, as we moved in rhythmic unison – two bodies connected as one, two hearts beating as one, two souls flying as one.

Sparkling fresh and sweet with a dash of green shimmering in his eyes – he became my intoxication for life, my Virgin Mojito. Lost in his arms, I found myself like never before as we made sweet love.

Four months later

"C'mon, hurry up!" I shouted into Ravi's ears.

Soon after breaking my promise to Mom, I had confided about my secret love life to Ravi, knowing he'd understand.

He was exhilarated by his sister's love affair and felt proud to have been chosen as a confidante. He had been my all time partner in crime, after all. Sharing and preserving my secret love life, he became my best buddy too.

Raaghav was as touched by Ravi's genuine love for me as he was amused by his maturity.

Eventually, he had bugged me to death wanting to meet Ravi or rather Saabu, as he liked to call him! Saabu was equally eager and soon enough we had planned our first trio date for which we were late.

Raaghav had already reached our meeting point – Gate No 1, Adventure Island. Only, Ravi who was riding the bike had gotten confused and taken us to gate No.3. Now I was urging him to speed up as the U-turn was far off.

He decided to play smart. Speed up he did but not aiming for the turn, rather for the divider. We bumped onto the wrong side of the road, as Ravi laughed over his smartness. But his laughter did not last long. Out of nowhere, there came before us a traffic policeman, signalling us to one side of the road.

We had been caught!

Getting off the bike, I picked up the phone.

"Hey, I've aged twenty years? When are you guys going to reach?" Raaghav chirped.

"Uhhh... Raaghav, could you possibly come over to Gate No.3?" I asked, eyeing Ravi. He was trying to calm down the over bearing officer, who was wildly angry at my little brother.

"Of course! Everything alright?" Raaghav asked, immediately concerned.

"Well... Actually we got caught by the traffic police..." I answered meekly as Raaghav burst out laughing.

"I'm coming! What did you do wrong?" he sounded amused. I could make out he was running; in all probability towards us.

"Let me find out by the time you reach here," I suggested, walking towards Ravi. He was standing helplessly near the bike, as the officer was now haggling with another pair of bikers a little far away from us.

"What's he saying?" I asked Ravi.

"He's asking for two thousand bucks!" Ravi said, through gritted teeth.

"What?!" I was shocked! Outright bribery in broad day light!

"Let's run away, while he's with them," I whispered to Ravi, signalling him towards our bike.

"Deedee, he has the keys..." he said gloomily.

"Oh!" I came back to where he was standing on the pavement. "Don't worry! Raaghav is coming here."

"But that's exactly what I'm worried about.... My first impression on him and I've been caught by the traffic police. What will Raaghav think of me..." He sulked, all of ten years again!

I couldn't help but laugh at his concern, punching his fatty arm.

"He really likes you, Bhai! And what he thinks about you is not going to change with this tiny incident. Anyways, we haven't done anything much...." and just before I could finish, I saw Raaghav running towards us.

And my face must have showed my emotions more bluntly as Ravi turned to follow my gaze.

"Yeah, not much Deedee..." he kicked a pebble, straightening his shirt as Raaghav just reached us.

"Hey!" he cooed into my ear, hugging me softly.

He turned to smile at Ravi who held out his hand.

"Hi Ravi!" Raaghav took his hand, while Ravi engulfed him in a hug.

"Hi Raaghav! Finally we meet...." Ravi was all smiles. "And what a way to do so..."

"No worries! Let me talk to him." Raaghav looked towards the fat policeman. Throwing at me a reassuring smile, he walked casually walked away leaving the two of us near the bike.

Fifteen long minutes later he was back with a pink slip in his hand and an amused smile on his face.

"Too much trouble?" I asked tentatively.

"Na, na... Not much! No helmets... Wrong side driving... Jumping the red light... Underage driver... No licence... No RC... Bike with Rajasthan's number... Just that, not much!" Raaghav said with a straight face. I gaped at him and we both turned towards Ravi. He was toying with his ears, his cheeks blushing in embarrassment.

"What a first meeting!" Raaghav bellowed pulling him into a bear hug. The three of us burst out laughing as I opened up the slip – it was a fine of a hundred bucks.

Wow! From a two thousand bribe to a hundred fine! Impressive Raaghav!

I looked up to see Ravi animatedly explaining to Raaghav about what had happened, how he had jumped the bike over the platform with such style and flair. Raaghav was all into his story.

I sighed as they warmed up like long lost friends. Raaghav and Ravi had instantly become BFFs.

We walked towards the parking, Raaghav's arm across my shoulder, as I smiled envisioning our beautiful future.

It was Raaghav's first entry into the family. And it had been exceptionally eventful! How was I to know that everything that concerned Raaghav and me was going to be nothing less but eventful.

⌘

We entered the house like two joyous kids returning from Disneyland. Raaghav had pampered us completely – video games, ice creams, burgers, more games, chocolate puddings and a boat ride, topped generously with fun and laughter. Ravi had gelled instantly with Raaghav, and not at once did I feel he was eight years younger. Raaghav was just a kid with him and the three of us had had a complete blast, right upto the point of winning the giant teddy bear at the video arcade – the one that no one ever wins. Raaghav won it for me!

As Ravi showed it to Mom, unabashedly lying and bragging as to how skilfully he had picked it up, I smirked as I walked towards our ringing landline.

"Hello!" I answered.

"Hello, Ira? Hi! It's me again..."

All joyous vibes seemed to be dissipating upon hearing the voice through the receiver. I took a deep breath, willing myself to remain calm.

"How many times are you going to call me up, Roy?" I asked my voice as blank as I could keep it.

"As many times as you'd want me to, sweets," he crooned dramatically. I cringed at the last word, clenching my free fist and teeth at the same time.

"I am not your sweets. And I'm not coming with you to the party, so would you please stop calling me up?" I could barely speak as all I wanted to do was to shout.

"C'mon Ira! It's a re-union. All your friends are going to be there... It'll be so much fun. Your mom was so delighted to know about it and you're..."

"You can take my mom if she is so delighted. I am *not* going at all," I cut him off, just before disconnecting the line.

Slamming the phone, I closed my eyes, taking several deep breaths to calm myself down. I had vowed not to enter into any argument with Mom and so far I had managed pretty well. But Roy had been making things difficult.

For the last two weeks, he had been calling daily, insisting I accompany him to our school re-union. Friends, party and fun was all a cover up. I knew him too well to understand his hidden intentions. He wanted to present me before the crowd as his girlfriend – something he had been unable to do since a guy had dared him in class 12. I also had strong doubts of him taking advantage of our solitude in his inherited car – a big black SUV.

My thoughts were just not agreeing to calm down. The deep breathing was slowly turning to huffing and before I knew it I was seething.

Just as I turned to enter my room, Mom's cheerful voice from the kitchen reached me like a spark, "Roy called for you twice today."

The apparent approval of the guy in her voice set me off like a bomb.

With all the strength in my heart, I walked up to her. How could she be so wrong in judging boys, despite being a mother?! I was ridiculed beyond reason.

"Mom, do you know what kind of a guy Roy is?"

"He seems like a sweet one..." she started, stirring into the cooker, what smelled like tomato soup.

"Mumma.... Listen to me," I spoke slowly, enunciating each word as if I were speaking in a foreign language. I had to be polite to her, no matter what. Raaghav had taken it as a promise from me – to be empathetic and soft towards her. It was becoming a hell of a struggle at the moment.

"Roy is not a sweet guy. He was the most spoiled brat in school, one who every decent girl feared to be alone in class with. He had the most tainted character and I'm very sure he hasn't changed one bit," I tried to explain in as decent terms as I could about the indecency of the character concerned.

"Well... people change! He talks so politely to me, always courteous. I don't think he's as bad as the picture you're painting about him..." she answered.

"I'm not painting a picture!" I said through clenched teeth, banging the chopping board before her, a little too harshly.

"Use this," I said as she was cutting the carrots on the slab.

She obliged, rolling her eyes at the same time.

Urrrghhh! I hated when someone rolled their eyes at me.

"This is what is wrong with your generation," she started solemnly, engrossed in her chopping. "You're all full of pretence. Vegetables will cut equally well on the slab, but no... You want to pretend using a chopping board."

I stood silent, my arms crossed, waiting for her to come to the actual point that she was trying to make.

"Now take's Roy's example... Why pretend hating him when you don't exactly know him. A guy can be calling you only for friendship you know. Not necessarily everyone has the same intentions, all the time...." she continued, suggestively.

I stood aghast! Had my ears gone crazy or was I hallucinating some strange talk out of my mother?! Was this the same person who had just months ago bellowed upon me that every man's primal motive is ending up in bed with a woman?

I could feel myself on the verge of breaking another promise – this time the one I had made for Raaghav.

"You should probably go out with him once... It's not fair to just judge without giving someone a chance," she cooed calmly.

That was it. The same words I had so desperately wanted to say in her face had just been thrown across mine.

"That's exactly what you should have done... gone out with Raaghav once. It's not fair at all to judge without giving someone a chance," I blurted out, cold as ice, sharp as stone.

And without waiting another second, I walked away, leaving her staring at my back. I could feel my nails biting fiercely into my palms from all the clenching.

Shutting my door behind me, I flumped down onto my table, my head in my hands.

Shit! What had I done? For more than half a year I hadn't mentioned Raaghav had at home. Things had been smooth, even though not perfect. But now this sudden reference of him... Surely, Mom would not take it in the best of spirits. I cringed as Raaghav's face crossed my mind.

We'll give her all the time she needs, baby. There's no need to force her into it. Trust me, everything will fall into place.

"You're still talking to him?"

Mom's voice pulled me out of my trance. She stood sad and dejected as if I had let her down again.

She made no sense to me, whatsoever. She had all the love in her heart for a buffoon like Roy but the mere mention of Raaghav had her crestfallen.

I sighed.

"No," I answered, mastering the art of lies.

She just stood there, staring at me through her aging eyes. For a minute I felt something in my heart melt for the soul before me – was it pity? Was it love? Was it agony?

I couldn't decide. Breaking eye contact, I pulled out my books, pretending to start studying.

From the corner of my eye, I could still see her standing at the door way. It wasn't until I had opened the pages, weird images of bacteria and fungi filling up my eyes, that I saw her leaving the room. She made sure to shut the door behind her.

I twirled the pencil between my hands, contemplating upon calling up Raaghav. I wasn't too sure on how to share this event with her. To think of it, I hadn't yet told him about Roy and his incessant calls. I had thought it to be too insignificant an issue to burden him with.

I didn't get too much time to ponder over the situation as my phone started buzzing.

'Raajeshwari calling'

"Hey..." I answered the call, pepping up my voice.

"Hey baby...." Raaghav's voice filled up the phone, all excited and fun filled.

Dr Green Eyes had long become Raajeshwari in my contact list.

"Reached home?" I asked.

"Yup, just there," he answered. "So how did Aunty find the teddy bear?" he continued in the best of spirits.

I hated to pull him down, and I thought it would be best to play along. Roy could be discussed later.

"She liked it a lot," I smiled, remembering how she had hugged Ravi, over proud of him having won such a bounty!

"And Ravi took more credit than anyone ever could for it!"

He laughed heartily, infecting me into a soft giggle.

"Saabu is great, yaar... You're a lucky sister you know!" he chirped merrily.

"Yeah... I know. He adores me. And so do I," I said. Just as I did so, Ravi's loud voice reached my ears through the walls, "Deedeeeeee...."

I smiled, murmuring into the phone, "Think of the devil..."

And just before I could finish the sentence, he dashed into the room. His eyes wide, his face in shock, his mouth open.

"It's Mumma!" he managed to blurt out.

"I'll call you back, Raaghav," I muttered into the phone, before stumbling up from my desk to follow Ravi.

Something was not right.

"Emergency please!" Someone was shouting in the front. Loud thunder crackled outside, just before it began pouring cats and dogs. The evening had just become more lightened up than before.

I could barely see where we were headed to.

My mind wasn't the best focused as I had would have wanted it to be. The extreme white lights being reflected from all over the sparkling clean white floors was not helping either.

We passed through door after door, and the hustle and bustle at the entrance of one of the biggest hospital in the city was gradually being replaced by silence and serenity. As we ran across, the man ahead kept chanting almost monotonously,

"Emergency, please. Emergency."

With a wave of his hand, he kept directing the people to give us passage. The hospital smelled fresh of antiseptic sterilization and I ran along the stretcher trying to keep up with the team of emergency doctors around me. Strong hearted I had always been and regular visits to hospitals during my study had strengthened me further. I wasn't afraid at all. I knew technically what was going to happen – how the surgery was going to be performed, how long it would take, what complications might occur. I was completely aware of each and every detail. My mind was completely in control because it was not ignorant of the situation.

Knowledge is power, they say.

And as a doctor in making, I felt powerful enough.

But it was not my mind, rather my heart that was in the mood to play games with me.

It was but natural I guess to feel the way I was feeling – a plethora of emotions raging within as if Pandora's box had been unleashed open.

We entered the big glass gates into the Emergency Room.

As the lights dimmed to a comfortable level, the doors shut behind us crisply. We took a couple of turns in the labyrinthine passageways that made me wonder how secured their primary operation area was. And finally at the far end of the corridor I could make it perfectly, the room with the small bulb hanging over its gateway.

The red bulb was off.

As the stretcher was pushed into the Operation Theatre, I paused, completely aware of the limitations that I was bound to – I would be required to wait outside. We had been holding hands, and with one small tug I was left with my arm extended. I turned around as the doctor in charge came up to me. Placing one hand firmly on my shoulder she looked directly in my eyes and in an instant I knew something was more than wrong.

"We don't have much time for the body to cope up," she began gravely.

"In such an emergency like this, we do expect a major amount of blood loss and therefore it would be helpful if we had a volunteer for direct transfusion, if required."

I completely understood every word of what she meant.

I took a deep breath and nodded my head.

"I'm ready for it. Please take me in."

Without wasting a second, she opened the door and gestured me in. I stepped inside a hall. On my left side was a small locker room and on my right was a lane with several doors on each side. Right in front of me was another big door, beyond which must be the operating area I assumed, considering the structure of the gateway.

The doctor signalled me into the very first room on my right – it was a cabin. Gesturing me to sit down she informed the doctor sitting inside that I was the Volunteer Donor. The doctor was already dressed in his scrubs and leaving me to him, the lady doctor quickly hurried away. To get scrubbed up, I guessed.

"Here are the papers that you need to sign, please," the doctor in the room said crisply.

"Once you are done with these, please proceed to Room No 4 down the lane. There you will find scrubs for yourself. You will also be required to put all electronic items into a bag and store them into one of the lockers outside on the left." I nodded while signing the papers.

"I should be joining my team now." He got up while completing the statement. "Once you're ready please reach Room No 6 at the very end of the lane. One of us shall meet you there for further instructions."

I quickly signed the papers, briefly glancing at the matter – it was all regular declaration and consent form, part of standard procedure.

Finishing the last sheet, I bolted towards Room No 4 and quickly got changed into the first pair of scrubs that I could lay my hands on. From the pocket of my trousers I quickly took out my phone, car keys and wallet and put them all into my handbag.

It suddenly dawned upon me that I should send a message that I would be unreachable.

Taking out my phone again I quickly opened messages and hurriedly typed –

In OT as immediate blood may be required. Phone will not be with me.

I hit 'send', turned my phone to silent, put it back into my bag and walked over to stuff everything into a locker. As I turned to walk towards the end on my right, I noticed the bright red light on top of the big gate. The operation had started.

Resting my head back against the wall, I closed my eyes. The operation was going to take long. I might as well fit together the puzzle pieces that were scattered in my brain.

Thoughts flashed randomly across my mind as I sat in the little room connecting to the Operation Theatre. How destiny had led me here was still beyond my comprehension.

My mind reeled back to the day Ravi had startled me, barging into my room with our newly won teddy bear.

⌘

"It's Mumma!" he managed to blurt out.

"I'll call you back, Raaghav," I muttered into the phone, before stumbling up from my desk to follow Ravi. I rushed into Mom's room, only to find her sitting calmly on the bed.

I looked at him. He still looked shocked.

"What?" I asked both of them, trying to keep my voice as unperturbed as I could.

"You didn't tell her?" Mom asked Ravi, to which he could only manage to shake his head in negative.

"Tell me what?" I asked, vaguely confused. Though deep within I was relaxed she wasn't having a heart attack, yet Ravi's zombie behaviour was baffling me.

It was only a matter of seconds before I found myself in the same zombie like trance as Ravi. She took a deep breath, before the shocking words came out, "I want to talk to Raaghav."

Fifteen minutes later Raaghav had called me up to state that he was going on a date with someone special the next day – the special someone being none other than my mom! Once out of shock at her sudden request to talk to him, I had given her his number.

To say that I was freaked out would be an understatement. Raaghav was meeting Mom for the first time and I wanted everything to be perfect. I had eaten his brains out, mentioning her likes – no beard, formal dressing, overt chivalry; and her dislikes – no perfume on person, no flowers as gifts, no getting late.

Raaghav, no doubt was an ace at it all, but my heart was trembling with anxiety. Hysterically nervous, I waited as they dated.

Three exceptionally long hours later, Mom returns home, surprisingly head-over-heels in love with Raaghav. All praise for the sweet guy that he is, she apologizes to me for assuming wrong about the charming young man, showering me with blessings at having met him.

All the doubts that she had against Raaghav had been wiped stark clean in one meeting with Raaghav. It was no surprise then as to how much she started adoring him in the consequent meetings to follow, which became quite frequent.

Raaghav and I did date a lot now that both Mom and Ravi were into the secret affair, but more often it was the four of us who'd end up together.

Well, 75% of my family was hooked onto Raaghav like a charm; they adored him. But the remaining 25% part of the family, Dad was still a big issue of contemplation. Everyone feared him in equally large proportions; everyone barring Raaghav.

⌘

"Uno!" Raaghav called out loud.

"Again?" Ravi squealed, half in admiration, half in shock.

"Yes beta," Raaghav answered, trying to mimic Mom. The four of us burst out laughing at Raaghav's funny face. Ravi rolled off onto the grass, clenching his stomach, shouting out to Raaghav. We were all sprawled out on a bed sheet in the park, just having finished lunch along with a dozen games of Uno.

"Please stop! Please I'm going to die laughing!" he screamed between bouts of laughter. I continued shuffling the cards before stacking up the deck, giggling myself uncontrollably.

"But what did you do? Some magic tantric stuff or what?" I asked.

Raaghav shrugged, beaming at me.

"It's just me, you know. No one can help but like me!" he boasted.

"That's true. You're a gem of a person, Raaghav." Mom agreed with conviction, patting his back.

Smiling at him playfully, I winked as he began dealing the cards.

I still had no clue as to what kind of a miracle had happened between Mom and Raaghav on their first date. It didn't quite really matter though now.

Raaghav had become more like a son to Mom now. In fact of the three of us, he was her favourite. So much so, that she finally agreed to get her pending uterine operation done upon Raaghav's request. I had been trying to convince her for it since the last two years, but to no avail. And Dr Green Eyes took just ten minutes to have her book an appointment for the surgery.

I was starting to doubt whether Raaghav really had some hidden magical powers. The next minute he confirmed my doubts, reading my mind yet again.

"So all set for tomorrow, Mumma?" he asked vibrantly.

"Inherent problem with doctors I guess," Ravi stated. "On one hand we have the two of you..." he said, looking at Raaghav and me, "...you're both so chilled out and cool, as if she's going on a picnic tomorrow! And one hand, we have Dad..." he sighed, shaking his head.

"Dad fears too much... He's phobic of hospitals and doctors! Not his fault, Bhai..." I tried explaining our father's psychology to Ravi.

He shrugged unsure of how to react. Dad had opted out of staying in the hospital during the surgery and Ravi was not convinced about his choices. I was only glad Mom had her trust in Raaghav.

"I fear if Papa gets to know all this! Secretly going out with you and being part of your hidden love story. He'll surely have a heart attack if he gets to know I'm so involved!" Mom said almost sheepishly. Raaghav was still top secret at home and Dad had no inkling about his affair with me. Or should I say his affairs with me, my brother and my mother.

I smiled, content and happy in the currently blissful phase of my life. For the moment, handling Dad was not of concern. We had a long time to prep him up and condition him step by step, all in good time.

How was I to know then that Dad's prepping would have to be sudden and immediate. The biggest event in my story was about to take place as I played cards with Raaghav, unaware of what the morrow was going to bring forth.

⌘

I walked out of the examiner's room, satisfied with my performance. The viva had been drilling but I had done well. Now, I had to rush back home. Mom was all over my mind. Her uterine surgery had been successful the previous night and she was expected to be discharged by noon. Raaghav had left early in the morning, just before Dad had arrived at the hospital. Leaving him with a slightly nauseas Mom, I had myself headed to college – revising for the viva en route.

Quickly finding my phone, I opened it up as I bid goodbye to others in queue outside the examiner's room. But hardly had I made it down the stairs, when the sudden inflow of notifications had me stop in mid track.

21 missed calls and 7 messages.

My intuition was back with a bang. All the messages were from Dad and the calls were a mix from the hospital, home as well as Dad. I knew in an instant Mom was not fine.

I dialled in Dad's number, which he answered even before the bell rang.

"Beta, Your Mom is not fine," he was almost on the verge of crying, it felt. Dad had white coat hypertension and his phobia was being tested to peak right now.

"Relax, Dad... What happened?" I tried to soothe him down.

"She's vomiting and has been crying in severe pain for the last three hours... They're saying something went wrong during the surgery."

"Hmmm... Don't worry Dad. I'm on my way," I said calmly, throwing my stuff into the back seat of my Tata Nano.

I had to reach the hospital before he fell onto another stretcher with a nervous breakdown.

"What do you mean by a minor cut?" I asked, trying to keep my voice low.

The doctor on duty was explaining Mom's condition to me but failing pathetically at it. I was a doctor in the making myself, and knew too well what blunder had been done.

"Please get me the release papers. Immediately!" I added curtly, typing in the number of the hospital that Raaghav had insisted upon instead of this little one. But Mom had preferred this primarily because of its proximity to home. I requested an ambulance and hung up just as I received a call from Mom's operating doctor.

She was all apologetic, pushing me to transfer her immediately to the other hospital. Apparently she too had tried convincing Mom into choosing it over this one. But who can win over destiny?

I reached Dad in the waiting room, searching for the right words to explain the situation to him. I couldn't put out the exact truth before him, yet I had to describe the situation as best as possible.

"The assistant who was holding the retractor, accidently slipped it which caused a small cut in her intestine... So, whatever she's been eating since last night is being spread inside the body through the leak. That needs to be repaired and she'll be fine, no worries!" I smiled at Dad, holding his hand tight.

He bit his lip, his eyes filled with tears.

"We just need to take her to a bigger hospital," I stated as casually as possible.

The fear in his eyes magnified immediately.

"No worries Dad... I'll come with her in the ambulance, you reach comfortably. Don't stress over it, everything is fine." Though my brain knew too much to trust my own words, my heart was in full conviction.

Fifteen minutes later, I was in the ambulance with my moaning mother. She was in extreme pain, her stomach puffed up to thrice its size, arching like a huge balloon through the hospital gown. Holding her hand, trying to calm her down, I tried Raaghav's number for the hundredth time.

It was still switched off.

⌘

I opened my eyes, coming back to the dreariness of the room. The red light was still on.

Though I had just been sitting, surprisingly I was feeling exhausted. I realized I hadn't eaten anything since the morning. I scanned the room to find a small water dispenser in one corner. Pouring myself a glass of water, I stood staring at the cover of the dispenser. It was a bright hue of my favourite shade – green. My mind reeled back to the blessed moment from the past – Raaghav entering Anatomy class, hitting my life for a toss with his green eyes; the eyes that became the world for me. My love for them and their dear owner had made me pursue a beautiful journey; one that had been full of love, emotion, commitment and understanding. It was a journey written by God's own hands. It made me luckier than no one else was to be blessed by a love as pure and as true as Raaghav's. I had only heard in stories about the power of true love and how miraculous it could be, until I had started understanding my journey with Raaghav. And now it was time for us to take the last step. In all probability it was taking place outside just now. Raaghav's meeting with the final person in my family – the veto power holder, the head of the family, my hero, my idol – Dad.

I had sent the same message to both of them, before locking myself up in this room. To Raaghav I had sent another one.

Dad will be here. All the best.

Dad was a man of few words, just like the average Indian father, I guess. He didn't express himself all too much and we kids had always used Mom as a medium to reach out to him. Not that he had ever overtly pushed us away, but maybe we never tried to get close to him, to know him better. Probably, that is what led us to believe him as reserved. Strict and orthodox would be two other adjectives that would definitely come along for him. He believed firmly in ideals and discipline – both of which were enemies to me. No wonder then having a hidden boyfriend at the mere age of nineteen, whom I had decided to marry was not an issue that would go down well with him. There had been only one other love marriage in our family, one that had to go through quite a battle. Now I stood on the verge of a similar battle, just with more complications – I was hardly into college and my prospective groom was yet to pass out. Settling into careers seemed as far as the moon, at least for me. And we knew absolutely nothing about our horoscope compatibility; a paramount factor in the view of our traditional parents. As I gulped down the glass of water, I realized the operation inside had lesser complications than what Dad could diagnose in my relationship with Raaghav. I was hardly anxious about the surgery going on inside. However the events that might be unfolding outside had me highly edgy. As I placed back the glass, the red bulb went off.

"The surgery went well. Everything's fine but we had to put her on ventilator," said the doctor, exiting the OT.

"She's being shifted to the ICU and you'll be able to meet her there once," she added, smiling softly.

I sighed at hearing the good news, thanking her, before heading to change back into my clothes. A different kind of news was waiting outside for me – good or bad, I was yet to know.

⌘

I switched on my phone as I walked through the labyrinth of corridors leading to the waiting area. But before it could spark up, I turned the last bend and stopped in mid track.

Raaghav was standing with his back towards me talking to someone I couldn't see. I took a deep breath and just as I took the next step, he turned his head, smiling as our eyes met. I smiled back meekly as he turned completely to reveal the person whom he was talking to. Sitting on the couch behind him was none other than Dad. He held out his arm for me as he saw him before him. I slowly walked up to them, unsure of how to react and what to say. Thankfully, Raaghav saved me, yet again.

"All good inside?" he asked as I reached them, gently placing his hand on my arm. I nodded, looking from him to Dad and back to him, before holding Dad's outstretched hand.

"She's fine. The surgery went well and she's being shifted to the ICU. You'll be able to meet her there," I whispered to Dad, who had gone cold as ice.

"Was blood required?" Dad tried to speak, barely audible.

"No... they got a matching sample from the blood bank just when they needed it." I smiled at him, trying to reassure him.

"God's grace is huge..." he whispered, bowing his head in a little prayer. "Raaghav donated his blood as soon as he reached here, making sure to inform the nurse it was for the surgery in progress. How can I ever thank you, beta..." His voice trailed off.

I could feel the goose bumps rising on my arms, as my eyes filled up with tears. I looked up at Raaghav – my angel for all reasons. I could feel my heart swell with love, gratitude, pride and joy! He kneeled down on the ground near Dad, taking his free hand into his.

"It's something I would have done for my mother and she is the same for me... just like you are a father. Please don't make me feel like a stranger by thanking me," he said softly.

"Now cheer up! Mom is going to be great. You really should eat something now that you know everything is fine. I tried so hard Ira, but now I know where your determination comes from," he added, trying to lighten us up.

I smiled at Dad hugging him partially.

"I think the word you want to use is stubborn and not determination," I said mockingly.

"Stubborn or determined, it's all about perspective. And I'm glad you didn't change yours for him," spoke Dad solemnly, cocking his head in Raaghav's direction.

I caught a small smile on Raaghav's face before I turned to face Dad. He smiled softly and I relaxed. In fact, I had never felt so much at peace as I was feeling at the moment. The last piece in the puzzle of my story had fit without any effort on my part at all. Dad had accepted Raaghav as if he had known him since ever. He had no questions, no doubts and no second thoughts about the choice I had made for the rest of my life.

Raaghav continued to convince Dad into eating something, handing him a sandwich and handing me one too.

I smiled at the sight before me – the two most important men in my life had bonded perfectly. To me it was no less than a miracle. Just as miraculous as it had been to find true love in a world where it had become a precious rarity.

I had been blessed beyond measure with life's most beautiful treasure – love in bounty from God's own angel, my sweet Virgin Mojito; Raaghav.

One month later

"Yummy!" I exclaimed, devouring the golgappas out of Raaghav's hands.

As I picked up another one, dipping it into the spiced water, Ravi came running into the room.

"Me too, me too!" he shouted, jumping around the bed.

"Relax, beta..." Dad said, trying to make some space for him.

We were all sitting in Mom's room, having a little party. Her stitches had just come off and while she was allowed only homemade daal and khichdi, the rest of us were feasting on our favourite street food.

But the celebration was not for her stitches coming off though. The reason behind the party was in fact Raaghav. I had been training him for the last two weeks and today having perfected driving a car, he had obtained his driver's licence.

"To Raaghav... the man who can finally drive up to meet my sister!" bellowed Ravi, raising a golgappa as toast.

"To Raaghav... the man who stole my daughter's heart for good," added Dad, raising another golgappa.

"To Raaghav... the man who saved my life," spoke Mom, raising her medicine cup instead.

"To Raaghav... For everything and more..." I paused raising my hand, short of words before my family.

Raaghav smiled, dipping his golgappa into the water, before raising it with the other dripping pieces.

"To Ira... for her unconditional love that makes me what I am today; the luckiest man on earth," he said, looking straight at me, the million dollar smile awakening the butterflies in my tummy.

"Cheers!" My family said aloud in unison as we giggled at each other.

Raaghav's spell was full on, and only got stronger with each passing moment.

The sweet concoction of my love story had blended to perfection – sweet and sparkling, with the right dash of green, it was without doubt the perfect intoxication to keep me high for life.

Jill and Jack found the perfect hack
For a life filled with love and laughter
Marrying each other, they kissed at the altar
And together lived happily ever after.